BETT   AIN BOOKS
45-

There's a
in Tyler,

And Molly and Quinn Spencer
are prepared for anything
EXCEPT:

Reunited lovers in fighting form...

The sexiest man in America,
trapped in the basement with the librarian...

And a bride who's begun her honeymoon
without her groom!

Anything can happen, and it *has*...
At Tyler's *Breakfast Inn Bed*

Three original stories by

Kristine Rolofson
Heather MacAllister
and Jacqueline Diamond

Y'S BARGAIN BOOKS
150 OASIS STREET
INDIO, CA 92201

Kristine Rolofson read and analyzed over two hundred Harlequin romances before beginning to write and sell her own first novel. Now the author of over two dozen books, she is the winner of the Holt Medallion and the National Reader's Choice award. Kristine lived in the mountains of northern Idaho for twelve years before returning to her native Rhode Island. Having married her high school history teacher at the age of eighteen, she has now been married for twenty-nine years and is the mother of six—the Rolofsons were named Rhode Island's Adoptive Family of the Year!

Heather MacAllister lives in Texas with her electrical engineer husband and two live-wire sons whose antics inspire her humorous approach to love and life. She writes for both the Harlequin Romance and Harlequin Temptation series, finding the main difference between her stories for each is that her Romance heroines find love, but love always has to go out and catch her Temptation heroines. But in the end, of course, they all live happily ever after!

Jacqueline Diamond began her career as an Associated Press reporter and television columnist in Los Angeles, and has interviewed hundreds of celebrities. Now a full-time fiction writer, she has sold fifty-four novels that span romance, suspense and fantasy. Though she was born in Texas and raised in Nashville and Louisville, home is now Southern California. She and her husband are the parents of two sons, both hardworking students!

KRISTINE ROLOFSON
HEATHER MACALLISTER
JACQUELINE DIAMOND

HARLEQUIN®

TORONTO • NEW YORK • LONDON
AMSTERDAM • PARIS • SYDNEY • HAMBURG
STOCKHOLM • ATHENS • TOKYO • MILAN • MADRID
PRAGUE • WARSAW • BUDAPEST • AUCKLAND

If you purchased this book without a cover you should be aware
that this book is stolen property. It was reported as "unsold and
destroyed" to the publisher, and neither the author nor the
publisher has received any payment for this "stripped book."

ISBN 0-373-83457-8

TYLER BRIDES

Copyright © 2001 by Harlequin Books S.A.

Special thanks and acknowledgment to Kristine Rolofson,
Heather MacAllister and Jacqueline Diamond for their contribution
to the Return to Tyler series.

MEANT FOR EACH OTHER
Copyright © 2001 by Harlequin Books S.A.

BEHIND CLOSED DOORS
Copyright © 2001 by Harlequin Books S.A.

THE BRIDE'S SURPRISE
Copyright © 2001 by Harlequin Books S.A.

All rights reserved. Except for use in any review, the reproduction or
utilization of this work in whole or in part in any form by any electronic,
mechanical or other means, now known or hereafter invented, including
xerography, photocopying and recording, or in any information storage
or retrieval system, is forbidden without the written permission of the
publisher, Harlequin Enterprises Limited, 225 Duncan Mill Road,
Don Mills, Ontario, Canada M3B 3K9.

All characters in this book have no existence outside the imagination of
the author and have no relation whatsoever to anyone bearing the same
name or names. They are not even distantly inspired by any individual
known or unknown to the author, and all incidents are pure invention.

This edition published by arrangement with Harlequin Books S.A.

® and TM are trademarks of the publisher. Trademarks indicated with
® are registered in the United States Patent and Trademark Office, the
Canadian Trade Marks Office and in other countries.

Visit us at www.eHarlequin.com

Printed in U.S.A.

CONTENTS

MEANT FOR EACH OTHER

Kristine Rolofson

CHAPTER ONE

"I HATE VALENTINE'S DAY." Gina eyed the pink carnations in juice glasses dotting the diner counter. Marge had gone to a lot of trouble to look festive and brighten up the place for the most depressing holiday of the year.

Marge herself poured fresh coffee into Gina's cup. "Isn't that a little harsh?"

"No." She was mired in self-pity and determined to wallow in it. "I'm twenty-three, I haven't had a date in seven months, I've gained six pounds since Christmas and I have nothing to write about for next week's column."

"My, my, aren't you a whiney girl this afternoon," Marge said, looking as if she wanted to laugh.

"It's going to be a long weekend."

"I assume that means you don't have a date."

"It would be a miracle if I did."

The waitress chuckled. "Now, Gina. You're

a very attractive young woman and you must know everyone in town. There aren't any nice young men in Tyler who look a little interesting?"

"Nope." She thought about adding sugar and cream to her coffee, and then decided against it. Maybe she should buy an exercise video.

"I don't believe that for a minute."

"That's because you're happily married. I keep telling myself that even if I met someone I wouldn't have time to date him anyway."

"So why blame Valentine's Day?"

"Because," Gina sighed, absently stirring her black coffee, "I'm twenty-three, I haven't been on a date in seven months and—"

"You've gained six pounds since Christmas," Marge finished for her. "I give up trying to make you feel better, honey. Do you want anything to eat?"

"I'm waiting for Eden, but she's late."

"She must be up to her ears in flower arrangements. That flower shop of hers will be doing one heck of a business this week."

"Roses," Gina murmured, picturing her artistic friend arranging red and white bouquets tied with satin ribbons and surrounded with green tissue. ''Bushels of red roses, she said.''

''Maybe you have a secret admirer who will send you some,'' Caroline, the quiet blonde who worked as Marge's new waitress, offered as she passed by carrying a tray of dirty dishes.

Gina laughed. ''If he's here in town he can just introduce himself and ask me out. I don't like surprises.''

''Neither do I,'' the waitress answered, surprising Gina with the comment. The beautiful young woman wasn't known for her conversation.

''Gina! I'm sorry,'' Eden said, rushing into the diner with a gust of cold air. ''I've been so busy—'' She unwound the scarf from around her neck and perched on the stool next to Gina. ''You must be starving.''

''It's okay. Marge and I were just discussing Valentine's Day.'' No one could ever be angry with Eden. Content with her garden and her florist shop, the woman was one of the most serene people Gina had ever known.

''I love it,'' Eden confided with a smile. ''You wouldn't believe the orders piling up for Monday. It's so exciting.''

"Anything interesting I can put in my column? I'm supposed to be writing something romantic for Monday and you could be my secret source for who is courting whom in Tyler."

"You know a florist is sworn to secrecy." She unbuttoned her coat to reveal a lavender sweater the exact shade of her eyes.

"You have glitter all over you," Gina pointed out. "No, don't brush it off. It looks good."

Marge set a cup of coffee in front of Eden. "Are you two ready to order? It's going to start getting busy in here."

"I'll have a cheeseburger and fries, please," Eden said, rummaging through her coat pockets before triumphantly pulling out a small box wrapped in white tissue paper dotted with glitter. A tiny red rosebud peeked out from the center of a silver bow.

"Me, too," Gina said, forgetting all about her plans to diet. Marge eyed the package. "What's that?"

"A present." She set it in front of Gina. "For Valentine's Day."

"For me?"

"Of course."

"It's so pretty." The little box sat on the worn

counter, its reflection caught in the metal napkin holder six inches away. "I hate to open it. Can I save it for Monday?"

"Absolutely not." Eden added cream and sugar to her coffee before nudging the little box closer to Gina. "You have to open it now."

She didn't want to open it. She wanted to savor it, as her one and only Valentine's gift. "Are you sure?"

"Absolutely positive. Open it."

Gina moved her coffee cup out of the way and picked up the box as Marge and Caroline paused in the middle of the luncheon rush to watch. She slipped off the ribbon, being careful not to injure the tiny rose, and tore the tissue to reveal a white cardboard gift box. She glanced over at Eden, who looked very pleased with herself. "Do I get a hint?"

"Okay." Eden thought for a moment and then declared, "It's more than what it is."

"Cryptic." Gina lifted the lid, unwrapped two layers of tissue paper and saw…a key. "A key? To what?"

"That's for you to decide," her friend explained. "I booked you a room at the Breakfast Inn Bed for the weekend."

"Molly's place?"

"It's gorgeous. You'll love it."

Gina picked up the key and held it in the palm of her hand. "This is heaven."

"I hope so." Eden thanked Caroline, who set plates of hamburgers and French fries on the counter in front of them. "You can move in anytime today after three and stay until Monday morning."

"Three nights?"

Eden smiled. "Of course. It's Molly's first Valentine's Weekend Special. She's still a newlywed and very high on romance. You can pamper yourself all weekend in luxurious Victorian surroundings."

"Eden, this is too much. You shouldn't have done something so...extravagant."

"You need a change of scenery," Eden declared. "And who knows? It's a weekend made for romance."

"Romance?" Gina laughed. "This is *Tyler.* It's not as if the perfect man is going to show up at the Breakfast Inn Bed to tell me he can't live without me."

Her friend picked up her hamburger. "You never know what's around the corner."

"In Tyler I know everything," Gina declared, pulling her plate in front of her. "It's my job."

"Just the same," Eden murmured, "you never know what can happen on Valentine's Day."

Gina eyed the key as she picked up a French fry. She'd been dying to see the upstairs rooms at Tyler's latest B&B since they'd been remodeled. She could write something about Valentine's Day there. Or do an article on the inn itself. Or she could start her novel. Paint her toenails. Pamper her skin with an avocado facial. "Eden, you are such a romantic."

"Of course I am. Your job is to report the news," her friend said, picking up a long French fry. "And mine is to provide romance."

"You mean provide *flowers*," Gina teased.

"Romance, flowers," Eden shrugged, and winked at Marge. "Same thing."

KURT EBER WAS a coward and he knew it. Oh, he didn't realize it right away. It wasn't until he saw the first sign announcing Tyler was thirty-two miles away that his stomach tensed. He kept pushing the "seek" button on the radio of the rented Explorer SUV hoping to find a station that would have decent music. Calming music. But when Tyler was twenty-seven miles away a violin concerto gave him a headache. Nineteen miles away he chewed two sticks of gum and listened to the news. Ten miles away he wadded the gum back in its wrapper and began to swear under his breath, not at the stock market reports or at the snow-filled weather forecast, but at himself.

Returning to Tyler sounded like a good idea two days ago. He'd been restless for months, despite Chicago's active nightlife. Despite the interested glances of the new assistant editor at the newspaper—a petite blonde who looked good in red. Despite his agent's talk of a television special. He'd poured his extra energy into his comic strip and was so far ahead of schedule he could easily drop off the face of the earth for at least three weeks without anyone wondering why he'd missed a deadline.

Which made it easy for him to say yes when his mother called and asked if he'd be interested in a long weekend in Tyler. Her husband, David, had surprised her with tickets to San Francisco, leaving her with a prepaid reservation in Tyler's new B&B. Would K.J. be interested in returning to his old hometown for Valentine's weekend?

Sure, he'd said, ignoring the *what the hell are you doing* voice in his head. And now, gripping the steering wheel with sweating palms, he wished he'd had something to use as an excuse, like having a broken leg. Or amnesia, so he could have said, ''Tyler? What's that?''

A few more miles took him to the exit off Interstate 90, where he slowed down to thirty miles an hour as he passed the Greenwoods Motel and Ingalls's F&M, the factory that still edged snow-covered cornfields. He drove down Oak Street and took a left on Fourth. The neighborhood was the same, frozen in time in the darkening afternoon, with its neat Victorian homes and sidewalk-lined streets. Kurt watched a couple of teenagers hurrying home for supper, an Irish setter barking at them as they passed his front yard.

Three blocks brought him to Ivy Lane, and he checked his mother's directions on the piece of paper on the passenger seat. He was to drive five blocks and then watch for a three-story green and white house with a Breakfast Inn Bed sign.

And there it was. He parked on the side of

the street and stepped out of his car into the frigid air. Kurt took a deep breath and told himself he needed the change of scenery. He would register, drop off his suitcases and then, before it grew too dark, he would take a walk through town to see if anything had changed.

And maybe, just maybe, he'd be able to put the past—and the most embarrassing night of his life—behind him.

CHAPTER TWO

"WELCOME." Molly Spencer held open the front door and ushered Gina inside the entry. "I'm so glad you're spending the weekend with us."

"So am I. Eden really surprised me this time." She set her laptop case and her duffle bag on the rug to the right of the door and peeked into the living room. "Susannah—my stepmother—said you'd done a beautiful job with the house, so I couldn't wait to see it."

"Thank you. Your father and Susannah have been wonderful to us. And your friend Eden has created some special floral arrangements for the inn." Molly smiled and introduced a tiny blond sprite who scampered into the room and eyed the new guest. "This is my daughter, Sara."

"I'm four," the child announced, holding up four fingers.

"I'm Gina." She smiled down at the child

and squashed a pang of envy. "And I'm twenty-three."

"That's a lot."

Damn right, she wanted to answer, but settled for another smile. The little girl grinned back.

"You'll have to excuse Sara. She's become a little obsessed with numbers since she started preschool." Molly gestured toward the living room. "Leave your bags here for a minute while I show you around."

"I've wanted to do an article on this place for the paper. It's gorgeous," Gina said, following Molly into a living room beautifully decorated with Victorian furniture.

"We'd love the publicity," she said. "We've booked all five rooms for the weekend, and I'm hoping that business stays good throughout the rest of the winter."

"Five," Sara echoed, holding up her tiny hand, fingers spread wide, to show Gina what "five" looked like.

"Are any other guests residents of Tyler?"

"Not that I know of. We have a honeymoon couple arriving tomorrow, after the wedding. The rest of the guests are here on business. I suppose they get tired of living out of motels.

Feel free to use the living room any time you like. It's for our guests to enjoy.''

"Thank you.''

"Behind the living room is the library, if you feel like reading.'' She gestured toward an open door.

"I like to read,'' Sara declared, tugging at Gina's hand.

"Me, too,'' she replied, tucking the child's hand into hers.

After Molly showed her an elegant dining room, described breakfast options, and led her upstairs, Gina figured she'd died and gone to heaven. The inn was a far cry from her third-story studio apartment on the other side of town. Her parents' B&B, Granny Rose's, had operated on a simpler scale. Here she felt as if she'd dropped into a world from one hundred years ago, especially when Molly and Sara led her into the Starcrossed room, which would be her home until Tuesday morning.

"This is unbelievable,'' was all she could say as she stared at a queen-size brass bed, its ornate headboard set against a rich background of bur-gundy- and gold-accented wallpaper. The windows on either side of the bed were draped in pale gold velvet with white lace panels that fell to the floor. The satin bedspread was a shade lighter than the wallpaper, and a rose, yellow and white patterned quilt lay folded at the foot of the bed. "Did the Tyler Quilting Circle make the quilt?"

"Yes. Quinn won the quilt in a raffle and we decorated the room around it."

"It's all so beautiful," she said, noting the soapstone stove and a container of split firewood in the corner. "And cozy."

"Thank you. You still have your key, I hope?"

Gina pulled the box out of her coat pocket and showed Molly and Sara the package. Sara's eyes widened when she saw the tiny flower.

"Can I touch it?" she asked.

"You can have it," Gina told her, sliding the bow and rose off the box to hand to the child. "It's my Valentine present to you."

"What do you say?" her mother prompted, and Sara stared up at Gina with wide blue eyes.

"Thank you. It's pretty." The child slipped the ribbons around her wrist to wear as a bracelet, but held the rose carefully between her tiny fingers.

"You might want to put it in water. It's been in my pocket all afternoon and probably needs a drink."

"We will," Molly promised. "As soon as we bring your bags up. Make yourself at home and if you need anything, just come downstairs and tell me. I'm usually in the kitchen. And there's a phone in the living room for guests to use at their convenience."

"You live here, too, don't you?"

"On the third floor, so we're right here if you need something. Don't forget to leave a note downstairs if you want to have breakfast in bed. I'll bring up a tray anytime you want."

"Thank you," Gina said, stepping farther into the room. "Breakfast in bed? I may never leave," she warned, turning to smile at her hostess.

"That's exactly the way we want you to feel," Molly said, and Sara waved goodbye before her mother shut the door.

It was a shame she had no one to share it with, Gina thought, surveying the room again. This was a place made for romance with someone very special. A burgundy striped wing chair sat near the stove, a matching hassock placed in front of it. It was the kind of room made for honeymoons, which made her wonder what the newlyweds' room looked like. She would come back and get pictures when she wrote the article.

For now she would revel in luxury, right after she got her bags and called Eden to say thank-you.

KURT'S FIRST THOUGHT was that Molly Spencer wasn't much of a housekeeper. He didn't have any idea how much his mother had paid to stay in the inn for the weekend, but he'd bet it wasn't cheap. Someone's coat hung over the back of a chair, a suitcase lay open on the bed, and a tote bag full of junk food lay sprawled on a marble-topped table.

On second thought, he decided he was in the wrong room, despite the fact that the key he'd been given had easily unlocked the door to the Starcrossed room, which was the one Molly had told him was his. Someone's silky blue nightgown lay in a puddle on the bed, and he briefly envied the man who was to join this lady tonight. This was a room made for passion, all right.

He took a second to glance around him, picturing the seduction. Heat up the woodstove and heat up the woman. Chill the champagne and light the candles. And, if this wasn't your room, back up and get out before some stranger belted you in the mouth for trespassing into his territory.

And before a woman clad only in an emerald towel stepped out of the bathroom and opened her mouth to scream.

"I'm sorry," Kurt stammered, backing toward the opened door. "I think I have the wrong room." He didn't stop looking at her, of course. No man would, not with that much satiny skin exposed. The towel barely covered her breasts, its corner tucked securely into her cleavage.

She said something he didn't quite understand, because his gaze had dropped to admire the long thighs below the hem of the towel before returning to her face. To a suddenly very familiar face. That's when he knew that all the gods were against him. *"Gina?"*

"Kurt." She fumbled with the towel, making sure it was covering everything it needed to cover. And then she stood very still, as if she was perfectly accustomed to talking to men when she was almost naked. Gina had changed.

"Wrong room," he repeated, his tongue thick and heavy in his mouth. "Sorry." She wouldn't have to know how sorry he really was, even if he had hoped he wouldn't see her this weekend.

"Obviously."

"Sorry," Kurt said again, still holding his black leather bag in his hand. He hated the guy who would see her in the blue nightgown. Who would take off the blue nightgown, lifting it inch by inch along those gorgeous legs of hers until he got to—

"It was nice seeing you again," she said, just as casually as if they'd run into each other at the Dairy Hut.

"Same here."

"Oh, dear," a woman said behind him. He turned to see Molly Spencer standing in the hall, an arrangement of red and white flowers in her arms. "I knew this wasn't a good idea."

"I'm sure mistakes happen," Kurt told her. "And you're new at this business, too, I heard?" He started toward her and heard the bathroom door shut. Gina had finally become modest again. "Just tell me which room I'm in and we'll forget all about it." He smiled, to show he wasn't upset. Hell, no. Just because he'd barged

in on the first girl he'd ever loved? The girl he'd
hoped he wouldn't have to face until he was
about ninety-two years old and drooling in his
wheelchair?

"Well, that's just it," Molly answered, mo-
tioning him back into the room. She set the flowers on a mahogany dresser, where they were reflected in the mirror and framed by candles in
sterling holders. "This *is* your room."

"I can take another," he offered. "Gina
shouldn't have to move." He hoped Gina was
listening and thinking what a gentleman he was.

"It's her room, too," the landlady answered,
this time keeping her voice very low. "Is Gina
in the bathroom?"

"Yes, but—"

She plucked a tiny envelope from the roses
and handed it to him. "This will explain everything, I hope."

"Wait a minute," he said, calling after her
before she closed the door and left him in the
room. "What's there to explain?"

"I'll leave champagne outside the room," she
said. "It's supposed to be for Saturday night, but
you look like you could use a drink."

He stood there while she closed the door and

left him alone in the room, with half-naked Gina shut in the bathroom. There was nothing to do but set his bag beside the dresser and deliver the note. After all, it had her name on it. But he paused, took a pen from his shirt pocket, and scrawled a drawing to the left of Gina's name before rounding the corner to stand before the bathroom door.

"Gina?"

"Why are you still here?"

"I'm not sure." He sat on the floor and made himself comfortable. "The owner of the inn just delivered some flowers for you."

"From who?"

"I don't know. There's a card."

"If you would go away I could come out and read it."

"I don't think it's going to be that easy." He slipped the card under the crack between the door and the wood floor. "And the landlady is bringing up champagne."

"Go drink it somewhere else. You're going to ruin my weekend."

He heard the sound of the envelope being opened, then silence. "Gina?"

She sighed. "What?"

"Who is it from?" He wondered if the man in her life, the man who was to meet her here, was going to be delayed. Or even better, had cancelled. Which made no sense, because he wanted to get out of here. He'd wanted to avoid the embarrassment of seeing her again and should be glad to pick up his bag and hightail it out of town, but oddly he didn't feel like running away.

He watched the note being slid under the door toward him, minus its envelope. It was a typical florist's card, and the writing was feminine and swirly.

Gina, don't be too angry. He's my Valentine gift to you. Do with him what you will, but try to work things out? You were meant for each other.

Love, Eden.

"Meant for each other?" he echoed. *Do with him what you will?*

"I know," Gina spoke. "It's embarrassing."

"Yeah." He sat there and thought about their situation for a minute. "My mother must have been in on this. I never suspected a setup."

"Neither did I."

"You're here alone," he stated, realizing with some satisfaction that Gina was not expecting another man to arrive and see her in the blue nightgown.

"You don't have to rub it in," she countered. "I'm here by choice, to have a restful weekend and get some work done."

"How can you rest and work at the same time?"

She ignored the question. "Could you just go away so I can get dressed?"

"No," Kurt replied, hoping she wouldn't hear the smile in his voice. "I liked the towel. And there's no place else I'd rather be."

CHAPTER THREE

"PLEASE," GINA SAID. She had to get rid of him. Not only was he the last man she ever wanted to see, but she was getting cold. And she was also feeling a little silly carrying on a discussion with Kurt while she sat on the bathroom floor and leaned against rose-patterned wallpaper.

She heard him leave, heard him walk across the wood floor and open the bedroom door. And then heard it shut. Thank goodness. She had pictured seeing him again someday, only in her fantasies she would be wearing something black and short and low cut, with black high heels and opaque stockings. Dangly rhinestone earrings, a perfect manicure and, last but not least, a "Do I remember you? Let me think" attitude. She'd dreamed of seeing lust and regret on his handsome face. She'd also dreamed that he was fat and bald and lived in a Dumpster.

Gina got to her feet and slowly opened the bathroom door. The next time she saw Kurt—who unfortunately was not fat or bald yet—she wanted to be dressed. Was that too much to ask?

All she could see was the window to the left of the bed, since the bathroom door faced that wall. She would have to peek around the corner to make sure she was alone.

On second thought, maybe wearing a towel—despite the added six pounds—was a kind of revenge. She hoped she'd looked sexy and not just scared to death.

"Here," Kurt said, holding out a glass of champagne to her. "It was sitting outside the door, as promised."

And he was sitting on her bed, right next to her suitcase as if he intended to stay for a while. In his other hand he held his own glass of champagne.

"I thought you'd left," she said, making sure the ends of the towel were securely tucked between her breasts. She had no choice but to act as if she drank champagne half-naked in hotel rooms every Valentine's Day.

"I thought if I did, you'd never let me back

into the room.'' He smiled at her and lifted his glass. ''What should we drink to?''

''Your quick exit.''

He ignored that comment. ''We'll drink to Valentine's Day. After all, I'm supposed to be your gift.''

''And as soon as you leave, I'm calling Eden and telling her exactly what I think of my gift.''

''Eden won't pay any attention to you,'' he said. ''Unless she's changed.''

''She hasn't changed.'' Eden was still calm and steady and quiet, all the things that Gina wasn't.

''You have,'' he said, studying her face. ''You look older.''

''Gee, thanks.'' Gina took a healthy swallow of her drink. And then another.

Kurt winced. ''I didn't mean that in a negative way. I meant that you don't look like a teenager now.'' Gina took a step backwards. ''That's a *good* thing,'' he added.

''Really.'' She took another sip of the icy champagne and tried to look as if she didn't care what he thought of her now—or then. ''Would you move so I could get my clothes, please?''

''Sure.'' He stood and went over to the

marble-topped table where a silver urn held the champagne and refilled his glass. Gina grabbed jeans, underwear and a sweater with one hand, careful not to bend over or spill her drink. More than anything she wanted to appear sophisticated and very much in control. "Take your time," she heard him say before she hurried to the bathroom.

She was dressed in thirty seconds. She'd forgotten a bra, but luckily her hairbrush and makeup bag were on the bathroom shelf. Her boxy navy sweater brought out the blue in her eyes, so Gina figured she looked presentable after she put on lipstick and brushed her hair so that it fell into a neat wave to her shoulders. Her jeans were a little tight, but maybe that was a good thing. She wanted Kurt Eber to think about what he'd left behind six years ago.

And she wanted him to regret it.

After she threw him out of the room.

"OKAY," GINA SAID, plucking the glass from his hand. "You're done. The game's over."

Just when he'd made himself comfortable in the chair, too. Just when he'd started to forget that he hadn't wanted to see her. Just when he began to think it would be interesting to stick around and see what the grown-up Gina Santori was like. He'd remembered a sweet, funny girl who'd thought she was in love and made him feel as if he was the luckiest man in Tyler. "I was going to build a fire for you."

"Thanks, but no thanks." She had the nerve to point to the door. "I can build my own fire when I'm good and ready to. Besides, don't you live in Chicago?"

"Yeah, but—"

"So don't you have better things to do than come to Tyler and bother me this weekend?"

Kurt thought about that for a moment. "Not really."

"Out," she said.

"But this is my room, too," he teased, pretending that he had no interest in staying anywhere else.

"This is not your room," she declared, stepping closer. She took the drink out of his hand and set the glass on a nearby lace-draped table. There seemed to be a lot of little tables in this room, he noticed, watching a very beautiful woman try to kick him out. "So it would be a very good idea if you picked up your bag and your coat and left now. Before I call the police.''

"Gina?''

"What?'' She stopped fidgeting with the doily and turned to look at him. Kurt had intended to tease her again, but he stopped. The expression in those blue eyes told him he'd gone too far.

"I'm sorry.''

"It's not your fault,'' she said. "It's Eden's. And I'm going to call her and tell her to mind her own business.''

"That's not what I meant.'' Kurt stood and walked over to her. He tried very hard not to touch her, though he wanted to put his hands on her shoulders to make her stand still and listen to him. "I'm sorry about what happened. Before.''

She blushed, which made him want to take her in his arms. "That's okay.''

"No, it's not. And I don't think it ever was.''

"Well, maybe you're right, but we don't have to talk about it, do we?'' She moved sideways and picked up his suitcase. "Here you go.''

Kurt took it, but he surprised himself with how much he wanted to stay here. With Gina. In this silly room. With the wide bed and the blue nightgown and the girl with the blue eyes. No, the *woman* with the blue eyes. "How old are you now?"

"What kind of question is that?"

"Never mind, I can do the math. Twenty-two? Twenty-three?"

"Yes."

"And obviously not married."

She walked over and opened the door. "Obviously."

"Boyfriend?"

"Hundreds."

"I can believe it." He hesitated in the doorway and Gina surprised him with a lopsided smile. Kurt didn't want to leave her. "We could have dinner tonight, talk about old times, catch up on each other's lives."

"I don't think that's a good idea." The smile was gone and he was forced to step into the hall.

"Why not?"

"I have a date."

"Oh."

"It was nice seeing you," she said, and then shut the door in his face. Kurt laughed. Gina hadn't changed; she still made him laugh.

"WHAT WERE YOU THINKING?"

"You didn't like the flowers? I put glitter on some of the rose petals for you," Eden said, her voice soft and unaffected by Gina's tirade.

"I didn't like the *man*," she repeated, wondering if the whole world had gone mad.

"You used to. A lot."

"I was young. I was in love. I was stupid."

"He hurt you."

Gina wouldn't argue with that. She didn't like remembering the very foolish teenager who thought she would marry K. J. Eber and live happily ever after in Tyler with little Eber children and a husband who adored her. "Eden, I thought we were friends."

"We are."

"Then don't give me any more men for Valentine's Day. This whole Breakfast Inn Bed weekend was a set-up all along, wasn't it?"

"Well—"

"Did Kurt know?" Please let her say he didn't.

"No. His mother helped me get him here." Gina heard Eden sigh. "At least talk to him. I don't think you've ever gotten over him, Gina. Maybe it's time."

"I'm over him," she fibbed. That summer romance had ended badly, though she'd thought they'd loved each other, thought they would always be together. She had just graduated from high school and K.J. had come home from college. Her mistake had been assuming that he was going to stay, that what she'd thought was happily-ever-after love had only been a summer fling.

"Then why have you found fault with every other man who has asked you out or been interested in dating you? You turn men down faster than I can arrange flowers."

She couldn't help laughing. "I never thought of it that way."

"You never talk about why you guys broke up."

"It's not important." Another fib to her best friend, who gave her a weekend in luxury and a bouquet of red roses and white carnations. "The flowers are gorgeous, by the way. Thank you."

"Don't change the subject. Find out why he left town—or do you know?"

"I know." And her stomach flipped over just thinking about it. What an awful night that had been. She'd thought—no, she wasn't going to remember the humiliation. "He didn't love me anymore."

"I'm sorry."

"Me, too. I thought it was the end of the world at the time, but I survived." And very nicely too, Gina thought. She had her own apartment, a college education, a job as a writer and her whole future in front of her.

"So, what's the harm in spending some time this weekend with Kurt?"

"Spending some time or spending the weekend?" Gina asked, pouring herself another glass of champagne. She would have to get some more, because this was really good. "I can't believe you thought I would be happy to be in the same room with him."

"Well," Eden hesitated. "I thought if you were forced to be together, you might work out whatever it was that caused you to break up six years ago."

"Oh, Eden, you're such a romantic." As if a few days could make Kurt Eber love her again. As if ordinary Gina Santori could turn into a sophisticated city lady and compete in Kurt's world in just a matter of hours.

"I can't help it. Say you're not angry with me."

"No." She took a sip of champagne and leaned back against the oversized pillows. "This room is really gorgeous. And you meant well."

"Where is he now?"

"Probably downstairs booking another room."

"The inn's completely full. Molly told me."

"So he'll have to sleep at the Greenwoods Motel."

"Or go back to Chicago," Eden reminded her. "Is that what you really want?"

"What I want," Gina said, "is to order Chinese takeout and spend the evening pretending that my old boyfriend isn't back in town and that my best friend isn't crazy."

She heard Eden laugh before she hung up.

CHAPTER FOUR

"TROUBLE?"

Kurt glanced up from the phone book to see Quinn Spencer standing before him. He looked as if he'd just come home from work, with his tie loosened and his suit jacket slung over his arm. A tiny blond girl had attached herself to his other arm as if she couldn't bear to let him go. The man smiled down at her before turning back to Kurt and extending his hand. "I'm Quinn Spencer, Molly's husband."

"I know you," Kurt said, taking the offered hand to shake. "You were a couple of years ahead of me in school. I'm Kurt—K.J.—Eber."

"Sure." Quinn draped his jacket around the little girl and whispered something, and she scampered off giggling. "You're the artist."

"Yes. I didn't know you were back in Tyler."

Quinn went over to a bar set up in the corner of the living room and took down two thick glasses. "Molly and I were married last month, so I've become an innkeeper, a husband and a father all within a few weeks. Will you join me?" He lifted a bottle of Scotch Kurt recognized as rare and expensive.

"Thanks." He tossed the phone book aside. "Finding a place to spend the night can wait a few more minutes."

"Did Gina kick you out?"

"You know about this, too?"

"Molly told me this morning. She said Eden Frazier had the idea to bring you and your former girlfriend together." He brought Kurt a drink and then sat down in the leather chair near him. "I told her it wouldn't work, no matter what Eden said."

"You were right." He sipped his drink, which tasted cold and smoky, as he expected. "Gina wasn't happy to see me, and I sure didn't know I was supposed to be sharing a room with her for the weekend." He couldn't help smiling at the image of Gina in a bath towel. "Not that I'd mind."

Quinn looked intrigued. "So you liked seeing her again?"

"She meant a lot to me," he admitted. "I guess she still does."

"So what are you doing down here?"

He took another sip of Scotch and realized he was glad he'd come home to Tyler this weekend. "Licking my wounds and trying to find someplace to sleep tonight."

"I wish we had an extra room to give you, but we're booked solid. We've had more business than I thought possible this month, and this weekend we even have a pair of newlyweds in what Molly calls the Double Wedding Ring room."

"I'll head back to Chicago if I have to." But the thought of spending the weekend in the city held no appeal. He wanted to talk to Gina. To explain. To tell her he wasn't the fool she thought he was—and even if he was, he could at least beg forgiveness. And kiss her until neither one of them could breathe, just the way they used to out by Timber Lake.

"Don't give up too soon," Quinn said, as Sara came running back into the room and threw herself into his lap.

"Mommy says dinner's ready," she told him.

He set down his glass and gave her a hug before turning his attention back to Kurt. "Sometimes you have to prove to a woman that you're worth keeping. And give her time to think it over.''

Kurt grinned. ''Oh, I'm not giving up. Not yet. I left my coat in her—our—room.''

''Well, good luck. I wouldn't be surprised if there are reservations in your name at Timberlake Lodge tomorrow night, just in case you want to impress a certain woman with a romantic dinner.''

''Eden strikes again.'' He stood and thanked Quinn for the drink before leaving his half-empty glass on the bar. ''I guess I'd better go figure out how to get back into my room.''

''The Greenwoods Motel can't compare to the Breakfast Inn Bed,'' Quinn declared, as his stepdaughter wrapped her arms around his neck and planted a kiss on his cheek. ''Good luck.''

He'd need luck, Kurt knew, going up the stairs. And courage. And maybe something else. He set his suitcase in the hall outside the door and sat to go through his belongings until he found what he wanted.

And then he made a Valentine.

GINA DIDN'T SEE the paper sticking out from under the door right away. She lay on the bed after having decided against putting her clothes in the dresser. Maybe she should leave the Inn, but the only place to go would be to her parents' house. Her landlord had said he was going to take advantage of her absence by replacing the ancient plumbing in the bathroom, so going home to no water wasn't an alternative. She wasn't going to explain to her mother that K. J. Eber was back in town because Eden had given him to her for Valentine's weekend.

Her father wouldn't be amused, but her mother might think it was a creative matchmaking attempt and would see Eden's point. Neither was a conversation Gina wanted to have, especially after having finished off the bottle of champagne. She'd turned on her computer, but there was no sense starting the article on President's Day, or the new columns on "Ideas for Snow Days" and "Where to Buy It For Less in Wisconsin." She thought about interviewing Molly's guests for a casual piece she could call, "So What Are You Doing in Tyler?" and wondered why the bride and groom had picked Breakfast Inn Bed for their honeymoon. Would they be interested in giving an interview? She doubted it—unless they might think a newspaper article would make a great entry in their scrap-book.

Yes, there was a lot to think about so that she didn't have to think about Kurt Eber showing up in her life after six years of silence. When she climbed off the bed to find out if there was a television hidden behind the doors of the corner armoire, she saw the paper moving back and forth under the door. She stepped on it with one bare foot to stop the motion.

"What do you want?" she asked, but there was no answer. She knew darn well that Kurt was on the other side of the door, whether he spoke or not. She bent down and slid the folded piece of white paper from under the door. It had her name on it, the lettering familiar, beside a heart drawn in red ink. She opened it to see three drawings, with the words "Pick One" on the top of the page. The first was a picture of a very sad artist trying to sleep in his car while dreaming of a long-legged woman in a bath towel. The second showed a young couple sharing a pizza. The third showed a long-legged man shivering in a snowstorm. "Be My Valentine?" was printed neatly on the bottom of the page, with Kurt's initials in the corner. She couldn't help

smiling at the way he'd portrayed himself—
skinny, awkward, with a large nose. He wasn't
awkward or too thin, and he'd grown into his
nose very nicely.

She'd always loved the color of his eyes, a
shade of blue much lighter than her own, with
gray flecks and dark lashes. And he'd had the
softest lips. She figured he was the best kisser
in Tyler, and she should know, after all the time
they'd spent out by the lake that summer she'd
graduated from high school.

Gina realized she'd better keep Kurt on the
other side of the door before she got sentimental and did something foolish. She rummaged
through her tote bag to find a pen, then drew
an arrow to the first picture, though she was
certain she hadn't shown that much cleavage
above her towel, and pushed it under the door.
And waited.

Sure enough, the paper returned, only this
time he drew a circle around the pizza and added
the word "Please?"

She liked the idea of him begging, so she
opened the door to see Kurt sitting in the hall
looking pleased with himself. "What are you
doing?"

"Waiting for you to open the door."

"Why?"

"I left my coat on the chair."

"Oh." There was no reason to feel disappointed. "I'll get it." She turned around and he scrambled to his feet and followed her into the room. His coat was tossed over a chair, along with some of her things, so she hadn't noticed it. "Here you go," she said, holding it out to him.

"Thanks. Now how about dinner?"

"I'm really busy."

"I see." He looked around at the papers strewn across the bed, the laptop computer humming in the middle of the mattress. "You've really got a career going, don't you?"

"Yes."

"So you don't stop for dinner?"

Gina usually stopped working for food of any kind—or ate while writing. But she didn't want to see him again. She didn't want to be reminded how much she'd loved him and how much she'd hurt when he left. She didn't want him to think she'd cared about him so much that she had never really ever given another man a chance.

Her eighteen-year old heart never quite recovered, but that was her secret.

Except Eden had guessed. And sent him back to her.

"Do you still like mushrooms on your pizza?" he asked, putting on his coat. He lifted her leather jacket from the chair and handed it to her. "Come on. We're old friends, aren't we? What have you got to lose?"

Six pounds. A couple of hours. Her heart.

"HE'S GOING TO BE FURIOUS," Janice told Eden. She hunched over her cell phone to block out the noise from O'Hare airport. "I'm surprised he hasn't called me to tell me so."

"He'll be fine," Eden assured her, surveying another arrangement of roses that was to be her last delivery of the day. She cradled the telephone receiver between her shoulder and ear while adjusting a white velvet ribbon. "We had to do something. Neither he nor Gina is happy the way they are."

"I'll probably be the subject of his next cartoon," Janice said. "Dressed as a witch." She heard Eden chuckle. "Are you sure this is going to be okay? Gina will talk to him, won't she?"

"Every room for forty miles is booked for the weekend," Eden said. "Gina won't let him sleep in his car."

"I'd hate to think of my son freezing to death."

"Are you sure?"

"Give them some time," Eden said. "Gina has called to complain already, but I could tell she was happy to see him. They're probably talking about 'the good old days' right now."

CHAPTER FIVE

"I DON'T WANT TO TALK about it," Gina said.

"Why not?" Kurt figured this was as good a time as any to explain to Gina about why he'd left Tyler. And left her. He might not ever have another chance after tonight and he didn't think she would get up and walk away from a mushroom pizza with extra-thick crust. He knew several of her weaknesses, and pizza was right there near the top of the list.

She waved her hand as if to ward off his words. "Forget it. It's old news. History. Six long years ago. I can barely remember that summer."

"Really," Kurt murmured, helping himself to another piece of pizza. He remembered those hot summer nights. Remembered her hair smelled like strawberries. To this day, walking through the grocery store's produce department made him think of kissing Gina. "*I* remember being scared to death."

Her fork stopped in midair. "You? Scared?"

"Sure."

"Of what?"

"You. Us."

"You didn't show it."

"Every time I touched you my hands were shaking." He smiled a little, remembering sliding his hands under her T-shirt to cup her breasts.

She blushed. "We were awfully young."

"You were. I, on the other hand, was old enough to know better."

"Know better?" She frowned.

"You were eighteen and all set to go to college in the fall. You were going to break my heart."

Gina looked down at her plate and fiddled with her fork. "What's your life like in Chicago?"

"You want to change the subject."

"Please."

He debated whether or not to tell the truth. Should he admit to loneliness or would that only make him appear pathetic? "I've been working on an idea for a television show for the past three months. I'll know soon if it's going to get the okay from a network.''

''That's wonderful.''

Not as wonderful as sharing a weekend with Gina Santori, he realized. ''Yeah.''

''Does that mean you'll have to move to California?''

''I don't think so, but the weather in L.A. sure beats winters in Chicago.'' Great. Now they were talking about the weather, which really was pathetic. ''What about you? Are you happy living in Tyler?''

''Very. It's not glamourous or exciting, but I like it here.''

''You've always been a small-town girl.''

''And there's something wrong with that?''

''Of course not.'' Gina was the kind of woman who brought laughter and enthusiasm everywhere she went, the kind of woman who fit into a place where everyone knew everyone else, the kind of woman who would be appreciated wherever she lived. ''So you're happy?''

''Why wouldn't I be?''

''I don't know. Are you involved with anyone? You told me you had a date tonight, remember?''

She shrugged. "I was trying to get rid of you."

"So there isn't anyone special in your life?" He knew the answer, after having seen her room at the inn. Except for the silky nightgown, there'd been no other signs that Gina was planning a romantic weekend. A woman didn't bring a computer, junk food and decorating magazines with her if she was expecting someone special to walk through the door and share the weekend with her.

"That really isn't any of your business," Gina said. "How many more questions are you going to ask?"

"Just one," Kurt said. "I can't get a motel room and it's too late to drive back to Chicago. Are you going to let me sleep in your room tonight?"

Gina had had enough pizza and enough champagne to feel that all was well with her world. And maybe it was time to make the most of the Valentine gift she had been given. Sometimes fate had a way of putting things right.

Revenge would be a sweet Valentine's gift, almost better than roses and chocolate and sentimental heart-shaped cards.

"Of course," she replied, smiling her sweetest smile as if she was completely unaware that the man across the table was staring at her dumbfounded. "I can't let you stay in your car. It's only ten degrees outside."

"Really?"

"We're adults, aren't we?" She didn't wait for an answer. "You'll have to sleep on the floor," she explained, sipping the last of her diet cola. "But I'm sure Molly has an extra blanket or two you can use."

"I'd appreciate that, Gina," Kurt said. "I never wanted to come back to Tyler, you know. I thought you would still be angry with me."

"About what?"

He looked surprised, then a little embarrassed. Gina hid a smile of satisfaction. She didn't want him to think she had thought about him all these years, because she hadn't. She'd put him out of her thoughts just as he'd put her out of his life, but she couldn't help wondering—just once a year or so—what it would have been like if Kurt hadn't left town without a word, without kissing her goodbye.

Without making love to her that night in August.

"Just one thing," she said, using her professional career-woman voice.

"Name it."

"You have to give me an interview. I need something for next week's column and 'Hometown Boy Returns' has a nice ring to it."

He frowned at her. "An interview? Why?"

"Because I came to the inn to work and, since you're here, I might as well make the most of it." *In more ways than one.*

"Well..."

"Please?" She leaned forward just a little and remembered she still wasn't wearing a bra. Good. She wanted him to think she was mature and sophisticated, so much so that she could casually forget to put on her underwear and not be self-conscious. "I hate to miss out on an opportunity like this."

"You're joking, right?"

"The *Tyler Citizen* readers would love to read all about you," she assured him. "You're famous."

"I'm not famous," he said, "but I don't want to drive back to Chicago tonight either." He pulled out his wallet and paid the bill.

"Thank you for the pizza. I'll have to tell

Eden that we went out for dinner and then went back to the inn together. That will make her happy." This was going to work out beautifully, Gina decided, slipping on her jacket. She would make him want her. She would make him regret what he'd tossed away. She would make him suffer before he left Tyler again. And then she'd get on with her life.

"HOBBIES?" HE ECHOED, shifting uncomfortably in the wing chair facing the bed. Gina, propped up with lace pillows, sat on the bed with the computer in her lap, her bare feet stretched toward him. She had the cutest damn toes. And she curled them whenever she waited for him to answer a question.

She looked up from the laptop's screen. "What do you like to do when you're not working?"

"I'm always working," he admitted, realizing he sounded very dull. "But the TV show should—"

"But what do you do for fun?"

"I run." He noticed she didn't type his answer.

"What else?" She wriggled her toes again.

"Are you still ticklish?"

"Hobbies, pets, friends, travel, sports, collections," she prodded. "Pick something."

"I like visiting old girlfriends in romantic inns."

"Stop joking." She yawned. And stretched. And he would swear she wasn't wearing a bra underneath the fuzzy sweater.

"I'm not joking." He stood up and went over to the bed on the pretense of seeing what she had written. "I don't think you can make me sound interesting."

"Of course I can." She didn't seem to mind when he sat down beside her. "I'm good at my job."

"I don't doubt it. What do *you* do for fun?" She smelled like lilacs, and the memories washed over him, hot and heavy, like Tyler in the early days of summer when the lilacs bloomed and girls in prom dresses hurried to dances.

"We're not talking about me right now." Gina turned to him, not seeming to mind that he was now making himself comfortable beside her on the bed. "Tell me, are you involved with anyone special right now? Tyler readers love romance, you know.''

He would have given up his last case of black pens to kiss her, and if he wasn't such a coward he'd kiss her right now. There was a teasing light in her blue eyes that made him realize she knew exactly what he was thinking about. ''There's no one special,'' he told her. ''Not at the moment.''

She turned away and began to type, then paused, ''Has there been?''

''Not really.'' No one he was going to tell Gina about, that was certain. There was no one in the past six years who'd taken his breath away just with the scent of her perfume or the way she curled her toes and frowned and typed at the same time. If he stayed in this room with her much longer, he would fall in love all over again.

''Too busy working, I suppose,'' Gina said, giving him another one of those quick smiles. ''How sad.''

''Kiss me.''

''I can't,'' Gina answered, still smiling at him. She took the computer off her lap and set it aside. ''It just wouldn't be a good idea.''

"No?" He reached over and tucked a strand of chestnut hair behind her ear. Her skin was as soft as he remembered. "What if you're wrong?"

"I'm not," she said, turning toward him as if they'd spent a hundred nights side by side in bed. "If I kiss you—or you kiss me—we won't be able to stop. Pretty soon my sweater would be on the floor and your chinos would be unzipped and—"

"And?" He could barely breathe.

Her voice grew even softer as she looked at him with those gorgeous blue eyes. "And we'd be out of breath and hot and I'd be on my back and you'd be touching me, you know, the way I liked you to and—"

"And?" So far it brought back memories that had never been far away.

"Then you would leave me," she whispered. "You'd drive me home and leave Tyler without saying goodbye. Remember that part?" He remembered, to his shame. A bucket of cold water would have had the same affect.

"I could explain, if you'd let me," he offered, wondering if she was going to shove him off the bed. But Gina gave him a tiny, resigned smile.

"We should let bygones be bygones."

"Or make up for lost time." And with that said, he leaned over her and kissed her before she could say anything else about what a jerk he was.

CHAPTER SIX

KISSING HIM BACK was the best mistake she'd ever made. Familiar and disturbing, unexpected and tender, kissing Kurt brought back more than memories of hot summer nights and teenage longing. Gina wanted to sink down into the mattress and keep on kissing until dawn. Kissing until the weekend was over.

Kurt lifted his mouth from hers...another achingly familiar gesture.

"Gina," he whispered, which was her cue to move off the bed as soon as she could get her limp body to cooperate. She pretended she didn't feel a thing and proved it by yawning, covering her mouth with her free hand.

"I really have to get some rest," she said, avoiding his gaze. She slid off the bed and caught her laptop before it crashed to the floor. "I think all that champagne made me sleepy."

"Gina."

"I'll go wash up while you fix your bed," she said, heading toward the bathroom. "I saw extra blankets on the top shelf of the closet, so you should be able to make some kind of a bed."

She didn't look back. Once safely in the bathroom, she turned on the faucet and splashed cold water on her face. She didn't look any different, she decided, checking in the mirror for signs of love-struck silliness. No, she looked a little disheveled, but very much in control.

Gina took her special nightgown off the hook on the back of the door and reminded herself that she was out for revenge. So far so good, because Kurt Eber had wanted her. And she'd pretended that his kiss was nothing more than a brief peck. Surely there was no way he could tell that kissing him made her skin turn hot and achy. Or brought thoughts of doing more together than kissing. She undressed quickly, then slid the blue silk over her head and surveyed herself in the mirror.

A sophisticated woman wouldn't put her sweater over her nightgown because the silk was too revealing. On the other hand, it wouldn't do to parade around in a slinky nightie she'd bought because the color matched her eyes and it was on sale. The sweater would stay on until she got into bed.

She would have to be very, very careful. It was one thing to make Kurt want her, but another to want him. Did the kiss affect her more than it did him? He was more experienced, he was six years older, he was a man who lived in Chicago and probably had lots of women in and out of his life. Falling in love with him would only lead to another broken heart, but she sure wouldn't mind if Kurt left Tyler on Monday wishing he wasn't leaving Gina Santori behind once again.

KURT ROLLED ONTO his back and groaned. So he wasn't forgiven. Not even close. Not even after six years the woman wouldn't forget that night out by Timber Lake. The night they *hadn't* made love because he'd been, well, too afraid to make the commitment.

And making love to Gina would have meant something. Would still mean something.

He stared up at the ceiling, and wondered what the hell he was doing and why he wasn't heading out the door as fast as his legs would take him. He never even called the motel and, with enough coffee, he could make it back to Chicago to continue on with his life.

But no. He was going to sleep on the floor at the foot of this woman's bed like some pet dog. And happy to do it, too, as the next best thing to being in bed with her. Was he still in love with the woman in the bathroom putting on that blue nightgown? He hoped he wouldn't have heart failure when he saw her in it. And falling in love with her all over again wasn't part of his weekend agenda, even though he hadn't known what Eden had planned.

Kurt decided getting off the bed was the first step toward self-control and sanity.

"Kurt?"

He turned, disappointed and grateful for the sweater that covered the top half of Gina's body as she stepped out of the bathroom.

"What?"

"The bathroom's all yours." She peered past him to the bed. "Did you find the blankets?"

"Not yet." He hopped off the velvet-covered bed and joined Gina in front of the closet, which she had opened.

"There," she said, pointing to a stack of maroon blankets. "You could use those for a mattress and cover yourself with the bedspread."

"Sure." Kurt wanted nothing more than to take her in his arms and kiss her again, especially when she stood so close to him that the silk hem of her nightgown brushed his pants. Instead he reached for the blankets. "I hope you don't snore."

"Me, too," she said and started moving things out of the way so he would have a clear spot on the floor. In just a few short hours she'd managed to make it look as if she'd lived in the Starcrossed room for weeks. Magazines, notebooks, pens and paperback books littered the floor and the tops of the numerous little tables that were scattered around the large room.

"I could build a fire," he offered, hoping that he could show off by setting logs on fire and looking competent.

"I'm warm enough," Gina said, stacking a pile of *Victoria* magazines by her bed. He was about to point out that she wore a sweater over her nightgown, but thought better of it, and watched as she folded the bedspread back over itself to the bottom of the bed, then tossed him one of the lace pillows. "Do you want the quilt?"

"Sure." He caught the quilt, too. "Made by the Tyler Quilting Circle, I suppose."

"Of course."

"Nothing's changed in town, then." He unfolded the blankets and made a mattress out of them, then fixed the pillow at one end and spread out the quilt for a blanket. Not exactly what he'd had in mind for this weekend, but more fun than he'd had in years certainly.

"You'll have to see for yourself tomorrow," she said, climbing into bed. "You should drive around town before you leave."

Before you leave was not a phrase he wanted to think about. Not when Gina was his date for the entire weekend, according to Eden. "Quinn Spencer told me that we have reservations at Timberlake Lodge for dinner tomorrow night."

"We do?"

"If you'd like to have dinner with me, we do."

"I'm really going to have to have a talk with Eden," she said, but she didn't agree to dinner.

"Do you remember our picnics?"

"Peanut butter and jelly sandwiches? I'm afraid so."

"And your mother's chocolate chip cookies," he added, pretending not to notice as Gina quickly pulled the sweater over her head and tossed it to the floor before sliding underneath the covers. So his Gina was still shy. "Do your parents still live in town?"

"Yes, but they gave up the bed and breakfast business. My mother concentrates on writing now."

"And what do you concentrate on?"

"My writing, I suppose." He thought her voice sounded a little sad. "Do you still need the light on?"

"I'll get it," Kurt offered, picking up his bag. He'd wash up and then get in that makeshift bed and try to sleep without dreaming of Gina. He paused as he passed the bed, surveying the very tempting picture she made snuggled under the covers. "Thanks for letting me stay."

She smiled. "I'll make up something wild to tell Eden in the morning."

"Good night." Kurt turned off the bedside lamp, which left the bathroom light to guide his way. He could make up plenty of wild ideas too, but fortunately he didn't draw those kinds of cartoons. These particular fantasies would remain safely in his head.

It was going to be a long night.

HE WAS GONE. GINA listened very carefully, hoping to hear the rhythmic sound of breathing. Or the shower running. Or footsteps. She opened her eyes and noticed some meager sunlight coming through the lace curtains, but she couldn't tell what time it was until she found her watch, which had fallen off the nightstand and landed on her sweater. Eight twenty-two. A luxury, even for a Saturday morning. Gina crawled over to the foot of the bed, just to make sure Kurt was gone.

Which he was, darn it. A piece of drawing paper lay on his pillow, which Gina retrieved by dangling over the edge. Her name was above a cartoon of the tall thin man with the large nose tiptoeing out of the bedroom while a voluptuous woman lay sleeping in a thronelike bed. The man was dreaming of the woman, while the woman was dreaming about pizza.

Clever. But where had he gone?

She'd wanted to wake up with him, but she

didn't realize how disappointed she would be when she woke and the room was empty. Gina crawled back under the covers, propped herself up with pillows and surveyed the room which, thank goodness, still contained Kurt's leather bag. Maybe he was downstairs enjoying breakfast with the other guests who preferred social mornings. Maybe he was one of those active people who jogged five miles at sunrise, or the kind of artist who was inspired by six o'clock coffee and the morning news.

Not that it mattered, she reminded herself, but now what? Breakfast in bed and a juicy novel or breakfast downstairs, collecting fodder for a future article. Neither choice was particularly appealing, so Gina rearranged the bed pillows and closed her eyes. She would have to plan her day so that she still had some pride left when the Valentine's weekend was over, so that she didn't get hurt.

The sooner Kurt Eber left town the better, Gina decided. She would suggest he pack, she would tell him she had to go to work, she would make up an emergency and pretend she had to pack, too.

The bedroom door swung open.

"Breakfast?" Kurt held an oversized wicker bed tray, most of its contents covered with a red-and-white checked cloth. A carafe of coffee—at least she hoped it was coffee—and two white porcelain mugs crowded onto the tray that was being carried closer to the bed.

"Hi," she managed, suddenly shy. It was one thing to share a room for the night, but it was another to be served breakfast in bed as if they'd done a lot more last night than kiss once. She discreetly adjusted the sheet to cover the bodice of the nightgown.

"Mrs. Spencer—Molly—suggested you might like to be pampered," he said, placing the tray over her lap. Then, moving the cartoon out of the way, Kurt sat on the side of the bed as if he delivered breakfast every morning. He picked up the carafe. He was entirely too handsome and too wide awake for Gina to deal with, so she tried not to stare. He wore a long-sleeved knit shirt and faded but neatly pressed jeans. How had he managed to shower and dress without waking her? "I see you found my message. Want some coffee?"

"Please." She watched as he opened the carafe and filled the mugs. "Have you been awake a long time?'' She took a sip from the mug he handed her. Molly had outdone herself; it tasted nothing like the black mud in the newspaper's coffee room.

"Since six. I took a walk." He lifted the cloth to show her the delicate plates filled with fresh fruit, scones and a wide slice of spinach quiche. "This is all yours. I ate downstairs."

"I think I want to live here for the rest of my life," Gina murmured, picking up a peach scone and breaking it in half.

"Food always was the way to your heart."

"Some things don't change, I guess," she said, shrugging as if to show him that she intended to enjoy her breakfast without feeling self-conscious. The sheet slipped an inch or two but she couldn't adjust it without looking awkward. So Gina took a bite of the scone instead.

"I've been thinking about what we could do today."

"We?"

He ignored the question and smiled at her instead. "I can divide them into food and nonfood categories."

Gina buttered the rest of her scone and tried

desperately not to fall in love with him all over again.

"Sara said there's ice-skating on Timber Lake now. I'd like to say hello to your parents and drive by my old house. And stop in at Eden's. We could have lunch at Marge's Diner and dinner at the lodge."

Gina started in on the fruit.

"Molly said I could borrow skates. She keeps extras for guests to use. What about you?"

"I have a lot of work to do today," Gina said, hoping she sounded convincing.

"That's not what I meant. Do you have ice skates?"

"In my parents' garage, but I'm not—"

"Great," Kurt said, refilling her coffee and his own. "Then we're all set."

"Look," Gina said, setting down her coffee mug and forgoing the quiche. "This trip down memory lane was fine for last night, but I really don't want to relive that time of my life again." There. She'd looked him right in the eyes when she'd said it. Even though it wasn't one hundred percent true. She wanted to relive it very much. But this time she wanted the happy ending.

Kurt gave her a disappointed smile. "I guess

I'm out of line. I guess...I've missed you and until I saw you I didn't know how much."

She melted. "Really?"

"Really. At least take me ice-skating, Gina. I've missed that, too."

"Then you'll leave?" She didn't know what she wanted his answer to be.

"If you want me to, but I don't mind sleeping on the floor too much." He slid off the bed and kissed the top of her head. "Want me to get you another scone?"

I'm out of line. I guess I've missed you, and until I saw you I didn't know how much."

She smiled. "Really."

"Really. Up until this time this morning, Gina. I've missed you."

"Then you'd better let me go so I don't know what she wanted her answer to be.

CHAPTER SEVEN

SHE KICKED HIM OUT of the room so she could shower and dress, but Kurt didn't mind. He'd come up with a plan for the day—for the weekend—and so far so good.

Two hours later Kurt wondered if he was ever going to get Gina out of the inn and all to himself.

"I should know him," Gina muttered, after they'd passed a tall, extremely handsome man heading up the stairs while they were going down.

"Why?" And why should he be jealous?

She turned to look back at the man, who deliberately ignored her interest. "He looks very familiar, but I don't think he lives around here. I would have noticed him before."

"I guess the Spencers have guests from all over the state. Maybe he's a tourist."

"In February? Who'd come to Tyler in February?"

"Me."

"You don't count because you lived here. And you were tricked." Instead of heading out the door, she headed toward the kitchen. "I'll ask Molly. Maybe he's famous or something."

"Can we do it later?" He looked at his watch. "It's almost eleven already."

"We can skip the skating if you're anxious to get back to Chicago," Gina said, and Kurt decided to keep his mouth shut.

Then there was a discussion between Gina and Molly Spencer. The honeymoon couple was due to arrive today; a businessman had recently checked out. Except for one of their guests cutting her hand, Molly told Gina, there was nothing newsworthy going on at the inn.

"How bad was the cut?"

"Quinn's older brother, who is a doctor, was kind enough to come over and take a look at it and assured me Mrs. Walton was going to be fine."

Gina looked disappointed. "Oh. The handsome man I saw on the stairs looked like someone I should recognize. Has he been here before?"

"He's a visiting businessman." Molly helped

her daughter down from the stool where she'd been supervising the baking of tomorrow's scones. The little girl waved at Kurt, so he waved back. "He keeps to himself, but he seems very nice."

"He looked like someone who didn't want anyone looking at him."

"Maybe he's an escaped convict," Kurt supplied, then groaned when he saw Gina pull her notebook from her bag. "I was only kidding."

"Well, you never know."

Molly laughed and handed Kurt a picnic basket. "Here's what you asked for, Kurt. Enjoy!"

"That's ours?" Gina looked impressed.

"Hot chocolate, turkey sandwiches and chocolate chip cookies. I told you I know the way to your heart," he said, and waved goodbye to Sara. Sara waved back and gave him a shy smile.

"Have fun," Molly called after them.

"We will," Kurt said, determined to spend the rest of the weekend—or at least the rest of the day—impressing a woman more interested in local news than romance.

That turned out to be easier thought about than accomplished, Kurt discovered. He'd been crazy to think he would impress her by ice-skating. A tall man with long legs did not take to ice-skating naturally, no matter how much he longed to skim across the ice while holding his girlfriend's mittened hand.

"When's the last time you were on skates?" Gina held him up.

"I don't remember. It was probably such an awful experience that I blocked it out of my mind."

"Think of today as more material for your comic strip," she said, smiling up at him. Her nose was red, and the blue knit cap she wore matched her eyes. "You can make fun of yourself."

"As usual."

"People like to read it."

"Do you?" His ankles wobbled dangerously, meaning he had an excuse to hold on to Gina a little tighter.

"Sure. When I have the time."

"Please," he said, draping an arm around her shoulders and pointing her toward the shore. "Such compliments will go to my head."

"Well, do you read *my* work?"

"I'll subscribe to the *Tyler Citizen* first thing Monday morning," he promised, taking careful gliding steps across the ice. The wind whipping their faces made it hard to talk until they reached the clearing at the edge of the lake.

"You don't have to," Gina said, laughing at his relief to reach the shore and sit down. "I doubt if small-town news would interest a big city guy like you."

He didn't tell her he'd discovered that everything about Gina Santori interested him very much.

"EDEN, THIS ISN'T FAIR," Gina whispered into the phone. Kurt was in the shower and she didn't have much time to talk.

"Why not go have dinner? How often do you get to eat at the Lodge?"

"That's not the point. We drove all over town and we had a picnic and went ice skating and—"

"How did you have a picnic when it's fifteen degrees out?"

"We were dressed warm and we were out of the wind—never mind that. I'm talking about tonight."

"Your picnic sounds romantic."

"Eden, everything sounds romantic to you."

Gina wouldn't admit that Eden was right. The day had been romantic and fun and very, very intimate. As if they were the only two people in Tyler, as a matter of fact. Her parents hadn't been home when she'd retrieved her skates and Marge wasn't working when they'd stopped in at the diner. Only a handful of teenagers were skating at the lake, which made her feel as if she and Kurt had the whole lake to themselves. They'd spent a lazy afternoon driving around town and talking about nothing important. She'd loved every second. Too much. "But this is getting serious."

"Really? All ready?"

"Quit teasing." Gina heard the water stop. "Look, I have to go now, but if I fall in love with him all over again it's going to be your fault."

"Maybe he's still crazy about you, too. After all," she pointed out, "he hasn't gone back to Chicago, has he?"

"No." But when he does, it was going to hurt. Hopefully only a little, if she was very, very careful. "But he will."

"Maybe," Eden said. "And maybe not. Have

fun tonight. Wear the black velvet dress you wore on New Year's Eve.''

"You don't think it's too fancy?'' She'd stopped at her apartment and picked up three dresses, heels, earrings and panty hose, which didn't mean she was going out to dinner but only that she was thinking about it.

"It's perfect. You'll destroy him.''

"I doubt it,'' she replied, before hanging up the receiver. She leaned forward to inhale the sweet scent of roses from Eden's flower arrangement. Here she stood, in the most romantic room she'd ever seen, while the man she'd had a crush on through most of her teenage years was now naked and toweling himself dry in her bathroom. She'd wanted revenge—or at least a little satisfaction. The black dress would suit her quite nicely.

Gina heard him humming off-key, listened to the unfamiliar sound of a man dressing on the other side of the wall. What was she going to do with him tonight? A more experienced woman might take him to bed, but Gina wanted love and romance, a husband and babies and a home. She'd always wanted Kurt Eber, too.

Too bad he hadn't felt the same way.

HE THOUGHT HE'D fall over when he saw her. The dress was black. And short, revealing exceptionally long legs that looked even longer in the black high heels and stockings she wore. It had long sleeves and a V-neck that exposed a hint of cleavage.

"Well?" The woman he barely recognized as Gina plucked her coat off the back of a chair. "Are you ready to go?"

"Uh—" was the only sound that came out of his mouth, though Kurt struggled to think of something mature and suave to say.

"Kurt?" She began to put on her coat, but Kurt moved quickly enough to help her. Her hair brushed his knuckles as he settled the coat on her shoulders and he leaned forward just a little to inhale the strawberry scent of all that silky chestnut hair.

"You still use the same shampoo," he muttered to himself.

"What?"

"Nothing. There you go," he managed to say, and Gina turned to face him. Once again she smiled up at him, which Kurt realized was something he liked very much. And would never tire of. "You look gorgeous."

"You look surprised," she said, laughing. "You've never seen me dressed up before?"

"Not since the prom," he reminded her. "Remember?"

"Yes. The night of my senior prom," Gina said. "Some of the girls had stopped at the diner to show Marge our dresses and you were there. You kept staring at me and I remember being very flattered. I knew who you were. And I knew you'd just come home from college."

"I'd ordered a cheeseburger and then this group of beautiful girls walked in and there you were, in that blue gown." He released a strand of hair trapped under her coat collar.

"Aqua."

He shrugged. "Close enough. I knew I wanted to ask you out, knew I was going to call you the next day and stammer about going to the movies or something. I wished I was a senior in high school so I could dance with you that night. I couldn't breathe when I looked at you. Like now."

"Really?"

"Really." Of course he had to kiss her, since he'd been resisting kissing her for almost twenty-four hours. She lifted her chin and met him, while six years slipped away once again and there Kurt stood, Gina in his arms, as natural as breathing. And kissing. And making love to the woman who made his heart stop beating whenever she looked at him and smiled a certain way. His hands cupped her face as he slanted his mouth across hers. He felt her arms wrap around his waist, his body reacting to the proximity of hers. Kurt didn't know how long they stood there in the middle of the room, but when Gina gently withdrew he knew he wasn't ready for it to end.

"I think we'd better go," she whispered, her hands still on his waist. "Don't you?"

No. He thought they should spend the rest of the night making love and then have breakfast in bed after making love again, but one thing in six years hadn't changed: Gina deserved more than a weekend affair. It wasn't going to be easy to remember that, though.

CHAPTER EIGHT

"YOU'RE NOT GOING to pull out your notebook, are you?"

"I thought I was being discreet," she said, looking across the table at her date for the evening. Dinner was almost over and she couldn't remember having a better time.

"You were looking to see who was here," Kurt said, teasing. "So you could put it in the paper."

"Well, maybe a little," Gina admitted, glancing around the large formal dining room. The tables were all filled, and she recognized some of the diners. "Timberlake Lodge is such special place for dinner and there are so many people here celebrating Valentine's Day."

"Like us."

"Well, not exactly."

"We're not a romantic couple having a Valentine's Day dinner?"

"We're just pretending," Gina said, smiling at the waiter who refilled her champagne glass.

"Speak for yourself," Kurt muttered before giving the waiter their dessert order. When they were alone together a few minutes later, he added, "I'm not pretending a damn thing. Are you?"

Gina took a sip of champagne, then set her glass carefully on the linen-covered tabletop. She would change the subject to something safe. "Maybe we should talk about the weather. It was awfully windy today, wasn't it?"

"Freezing. You wore that dress to torture me, didn't you?"

Gina smiled. "Of course."

"It's working."

"It was Eden's idea." She was secretly pleased that he seemed so rattled by the way she looked. So Kurt wasn't looking at her as if she was a teenager anymore? Life was good, as long as she didn't spill anything on the velvet. "I think it's going to snow again."

"Good."

"Good?" she echoed. "Why?"

"You wouldn't toss me out of your room into a blizzard."

"I thought you were going back to Chicago tonight."

He didn't respond. "Did I tell you how beautiful you look tonight?"

"Several times." She could feel herself blushing and pretended to look around the room again. A fire burned in the enormous stone fireplace nearby, adding another layer of heat to her skin, so she picked up her water glass and took a sip.

"I ran into Rick Travis while you were getting all dressed up to torture me."

"Was he in high school with you?"

"We graduated together. He went on to play football in college and in the pros until he got hurt and had to retire early."

"What is he doing in Tyler?"

"Off the record?"

She sighed, sensing a good story evaporating into thin air. "Sure. Off the record."

"He's here with the bride hiding out in the honeymoon suite."

"Rick Travis is *married*? Why would that be a secret?"

"He didn't marry the bride. Someone else was supposed to, but something happened at the last minute and she ran away. I guess Rick is one of her best friends, so he followed her here and is helping her out.''

''The poor bride must feel terrible.'' The waiter refilled the champagne before leaving them alone again. ''Here I thought your dumping me was the worst thing I'd ever been through, but at least I wasn't wearing a wedding dress and waiting for 'Here Comes the Bride' to start playing on the church organ.''

''I didn't dump you,'' Kurt said.

''You didn't?'' Funny, it had felt like that. She'd cried for three days after she heard he'd left Tyler to take a job in Chicago. And then she'd waited for the phone to ring. And the mailman to bring a letter. Her parents had watched with concerned expressions, her friends urged her to get over him and date someone else.

''I had to go.''

''You left town without a word. You left before—''

''Before making love to you,'' he finished for her, and Gina looked down into her champagne glass. She took a deep breath before lifting her gaze to his.

"Was the thought of that so horrible?" It had been the most humiliating night of her life.

"You know it wasn't."

"No," she said carefully. "I don't."

"You thought I didn't want to?" Her silence told him that was exactly what she'd thought. "Oh, I wanted to, but I was scared to death."

"Of what?"

"You. Us. The future." He leaned forward and took one of her hands in his. "I didn't want to stay in Tyler. I didn't want to settle down." His thumb gently rubbed hers. "And being with you meant *staying* with you." His smile was a little lopsided. "Old-fashioned, huh?"

"I wish you'd told me."

"Would you have understood? You were only eighteen with college ahead of you. I couldn't picture us together. Not then."

"I was in love with you the entire summer," she said, giving him a smile to show that she was over him. "And I wanted so badly for you to make love to me."

"Past tense?"

"I was young and you were my first love," she reminded him, unwilling to answer his question. "And I didn't know any better." She withdrew her hand from his as the waiter deposited their desserts and, noting the empty bottle, inquired as to whether they would like more champagne.

"Yes," Kurt answered, not taking his gaze from Gina's face. She looked away, toward the dance floor on the other side of the room, where couples gathered as a small band began to play something slow and romantic.

"You haven't forgiven me," he stated. "You're not going to make me get down on my knees, are you?"

"No," she replied, eyeing the slice of rich triple chocolate cake in front of her. "Because I'd rather have dessert than watch you grovel."

"I didn't offer to grovel," Kurt said, picking up his own fork and attacking a portion of strawberry shortcake. "But I was prepared to beg for another chance."

"You're only allowed one," Gina told him, relieved that he was joking again. "I've never had so much champagne in twenty-four hours," Gina murmured. "I could get used to this lifestyle."

"Yeah," he said. "Me, too."

"Don't you go out a lot in Chicago?"

"I didn't mean Chicago. I meant being with you."

"Oh." She tried to concentrate on taking another bite of dessert.

"I really did want to make love to you, Gina. You have to know that."

"Could we talk about something else now?"

"Sure. How's your cake?"

"Delicious."

"And the champagne?"

"Bubbly."

"The music?"

"Very romantic."

He seemed to hesitate, then, "And your heart?"

"In one piece, thank you." Gina smiled. "Don't worry, you're forgiven. We were young and stupid—or at least *you* were stupid—" She watched him start to smile. "Six years is a very long time, so let's forget it, shall we?"

He shook his head. "I don't think so, not when I want you so much."

"You do?" Oh, sweet revenge. The outfit had worked. She would call Eden in the morning and say thank-you.

"More than ever, damn it." He refilled their

glasses and frowned at her. "And you're going to make me sleep on the floor again, aren't you?"

She grinned, pleased with the world and a bit dizzy from the champagne. "Of course I am. You broke my heart, K. J. Eber."

He lifted his glass as if to toast her. "I've missed you, Gina Santori."

"Really?"

"No lie." He winked at her. "I haven't had this much fun in years."

"Me, either." She clicked her glass against his a little too hard and champagne splashed onto their fingers. "Oops."

"Maybe I should take you home," he said. "Or we should order coffee."

She shook her head. "Not yet. We have to dance."

"I'm not a very good dancer," he said, looking uncomfortable as he glanced over his shoulder at the band, then back to Gina. "I might step on your feet."

"You owe me," she said, wiping the spilled wine from her fingers before tossing the napkin on the table.

"A dance?"

Gina smiled. "A seduction."

"You're trying to torture me, right? Okay, I deserve it." He stood and held out his hand to her. "Don't say I didn't warn you."

He led her onto the dance floor and took her in his arms. She didn't remember dancing with him that summer. Walking, talking, kissing, swimming. Not dancing.

"Should I count the steps for you?" she teased, realizing he could dance quite well and it didn't make any difference anyway, as long as she was in his arms.

"That would be very helpful."

"One-two-three," she said softly, as he gathered her closer. "How's that?"

"Perfect."

"You're not going to run away again, are you?" She felt his arms tighten around her, pulling her close and he bent down to whisper in her ear.

"You said I owed you a seduction. Is this what you had in mind?"

Gina snuggled closer, knowing all the gods of Valentine's Day were on her side. He was hers, at least for tonight. "So far so good."

CHAPTER NINE

THEY DANCED UNTIL Gina's feet ached in the high heels and she kicked them off under the table during the band's break. They danced until they were barely dancing, but holding each other and shifting their feet in time to the music. They danced until the music ended with a dreamy rendition of "Good Night Sweetheart," the champagne was gone and the candles that decorated the tabletops were extinguished by weary waiters.

Kurt drove her back to the inn, which stood quiet and dark, a light left on in the hall to guide guests upstairs safely. Gina, shoes in hand, tiptoed up the stairs while Kurt tried hard to walk softly. Somewhere on the second floor was a runaway bride, an ex-football player, a handsome and possibly famous businessman, and a woman who'd injured her hand today. He didn't think any of them would appreciate being awakened by a cartoonist and a tipsy reporter who hadn't decided yet how this evening would end.

He hesitated at the door. If he went inside they would make love. Or come pretty damn close. Which, he thought wryly, was why she'd been angry with him for the past six years.

"I was right, you know," he whispered, as she unlocked the door to the Starcrossed room and stepped inside.

"Shh," Gina said, waiting until he was inside the room before shutting the door with a quiet click. "Right about what?"

"I was right to stop from making love to an eighteen-year-old girl," Kurt said, watching as Gina took off her coat and tossed it over the back of the wing chair. He stepped over her shoes, abandoned in the middle of a rug, and thought about hanging up her coat for her, but instead he threw his own jacket on the chair, too. A few more days with Gina and he'd have forgotten every tidy habit his mother had taught him. And he'd live happily ever after in chaos, Kurt realized.

"I thought you didn't want me," she said, turning her back to him and lifting her hair. "Would you get this zipper, please?"

He gulped, then fumbled with the tiny metal tab until he unzipped the dress down to the horizontal scrap of black lace that hooked the pieces of her bra together.

"I wanted you," he managed to say, dropping his hands as if he'd burned them. He wanted to slide his hands underneath the velvet and feel that satin skin under his palms. "But you were a virgin and I knew I was going to get a job in Chicago and it didn't—"

She turned around and looked up at him. "I still am."

"Am what?"

"A virgin," she replied, as easily as if she had told him the month was February and it was cold out. "You look upset. Is there something wrong with that?"

"No. I mean, I'm not upset," he said. Gina was his after all, and the relief he felt knowing that surprised him into realizing there was a lot he needed to think about. But not now. "You're waiting until you're married?"

She shook her head. "I suppose I've been waiting for you."

He should have been afraid, he realized hours later, when he'd greeted the dawn, had several cups of coffee and plenty of time to think. Instead of fear there was only desire for both of them, because his Gina smiled up at him and Kurt knew he was in love with her, had always been in love with her. And couldn't resist her now.

He wanted to be gentle, intended to take it slow, but Gina was as passionate as he remembered. The teenager who had kissed him in the front seat of his car so many years ago was now a beautiful woman who, with trembling fingers, touched his face and then took his hand. He didn't know who led whom to the quilt-covered bed, but this time there would be no turning back, no second thoughts.

A stone statue couldn't have resisted Gina Santori. Not when she slid the little black dress past her shoulders and over her hips. Not when she looked at him with an expression that made him fall even deeper in love with her than he'd ever been before this moment.

And when Kurt knew that this time making love to Gina wouldn't be something to regret, but something to remember.

TWICE, GINA REMEMBERED, turning on her side to snuggle deeper into the pillows. She kept her

eyes closed against the morning light and tried
to go back to sleep. He'd made love with her
twice, and it had been wonderful.

Better than in any of her fantasies, because
this had been real. With Kurt. The man she'd
never stopped loving.

Obviously.

She smiled to herself and stretched out one
leg, hoping to make contact with one of his, but
the bed was empty no matter how far she moved
her foot into the other half of the bed. He would
return with coffee and food, just as he had yesterday. Gina thought about waking up, but her
contented body betrayed her into sleep once
again. She smiled in her sleep and dreamt of
champagne glasses filled with strawberries, until
she woke again and realized that Kurt—and his
coat, suitcase and shaving kit—were gone.

KURT SAT IN HIS CAR, the engine running to blast
heated air through the vents, and sipped coffee
he'd bought at the diner. He'd forgotten how
cold Tyler could be on a February morning, but
after last night he needed winter's equivalent to
a cold shower.

What had he been thinking? With his gloved

hand he rubbed the condensation from the car window and looked once more at the two-story Victorian-style house in which he'd grown up. He'd left town six years ago and eagerly faced a future as a cartoonist, an artist. He'd never pictured coming back to Tyler and settling down, but spending the night with Gina had changed everything. He just didn't know what to do next. Could his life really have changed this much in less than forty-eight hours?

He pictured Gina waking up...alone. He hoped she'd sleep late this morning. In fact, he was counting on it.

"AND ANOTHER ONE OF those mysterious gift deliveries arrived yesterday," Molly said, refilling Gina's coffee cup. "You should do an article about it for the newspaper."

"No one seems to know anything about it, not even Eden," Gina said, trying not to look at the doorway that led to the hall. She expected Kurt to walk into the dining room any minute now. He was certain to have a perfectly reasonable explanation for having disappeared during the early hours of the morning. And a believable reason for staying away from the inn until almost noon.

"Have another," her hostess said, offering her the basket filled with apple-cinnamon muffins. "It's very quiet around here this morning. I'm going to ask Quinn to build up the fire in the living room. I think it's going to snow."

"Snow? Really?" Gina pretended to listen to Molly's cheerful conversation as she set the basket of muffins on the table and drank her coffee, even though her stomach felt a little queasy. When Molly paused to look out the window for any approaching snowflakes, Gina decided to make her escape. "Molly, I'm going to be checking out today. I have so much work to do before Monday and—"

"But your Valentine's weekend doesn't end until tomorrow, on Valentine's Day. Is everything all right with your room?" Molly looked so disappointed that Gina almost relented, just so she wouldn't hurt the woman's feelings.

"Oh, the room is beautiful. It was a perfect weekend," Gina lied, hoping she looked sincere and content. "I hate to have it end so soon, but I think I'd better get back to reality before I get used to living in such luxury."

Molly, gracious innkeeper that she was, accepted the explanation and wished her good luck with her work.

Once back in the Starcrossed room, Gina avoided looking at the rumpled bed where she'd spent some of the very best and most thrilling hours of her life, and quickly shoved her belongings into her suitcase and tote bags. With her laptop in its backpack hanging from her shoulder, she managed to gather everything in her arms and avoid making two trips downstairs.

She thanked Molly again, waved to Sara and smiled blithely at Quinn Spencer's raised eyebrows as she hurried past as if she were late for a plane. The cold air blew her breath back in her face as she hurried to her car parked at the side of the house, and as she dumped her things in the trunk, tiny icy snowflakes stung her face. It was enough to make a woman want to move to Florida and join a convent.

No wonder she hated Valentine's Day so much. Look what it had done to her.

"SHE LEFT? WHY?" KURT stood in the opened doorway of the Starcrossed room and watched Molly begin to clean.

"She said she had a lot of work to do," Molly said, busy piling up the bedding.

"Did she leave a message for me?"

"Not that I know of, Kurt, but please come in and look around. I can do this cleaning later." She shot him a questioning look as she started tossing pillows onto the maroon chair. "Are you going to check out early, too?"

"I'm not sure," he said, knowing he'd stayed away from Gina too long. He'd had plenty to do, to make sure this was all going to work. And he thought Gina would sleep late, especially after not getting much sleep last night.

"Well, I hope you stay until tomorrow. I don't want to lose both my guests today." She bent down and retrieved a piece of paper. "Is this what you're looking for?" She held it out without looking at it, and Kurt crossed the room in quick strides to get it.

"Thanks," he said, looking at the drawing carefully before putting it in his pocket. "Where did you find it?"

"I think it must have been tucked into the pillows," Molly said. "Is it a Valentine?"

"Yes," Kurt replied. "That's exactly what it is." He'd left it for her and she'd left it behind.

Which, considering Gina, meant only one thing.

SHE WOULD TELL Eden tomorrow. Or maybe next week. Eden would be so busy creating romantic bouquets to be delivered to various lucky-in-love Tyler residents that she wouldn't notice if her best friend was quietly licking her wounds in her tiny studio apartment and hiding her broken heart from the world.

Gina turned on the bathroom faucet, which actually worked, and splashed water on her face to rinse off the tearstains. She'd have to remember to thank the landlord. She'd have to spend the afternoon coming up with a column for Monday. Famous cartoonists and romantic bed and breakfast inns were not going to be topics, however. And she couldn't remember who danced with whom at Timber Lake last night; she'd only had eyes for Kurt.

Her cluttered apartment needed cleaning. Her books needed organizing and there was a two-foot stack of papers to be filed. So Gina, fully clothed in jeans and a sweatshirt, crawled into bed and took a nap.

THE POUNDING ON THE door woke her a short time later, and she sat up, groggy and confused. A piece of paper sat on the wood floor in front of her door, but she tried not to get her hopes up. What she hoped would be Kurt's cartoon could easily be the latest directive from the landlord.

"I'm coming," she called, hurrying to the door. The knocking stopped, so she picked up the paper and turned it over to see Kurt's familiar penned figure. This time the character carried a bouquet of roses. In the dialogue cloud above his head were pictures of a house, picket fence, wedding ring and a four-poster bed. Printed neatly underneath the cartoon figure's feet were the words Will You Marry Me?

She flung open the door to see him standing there, waiting for her. "I thought you went back to Chicago."

"You haven't answered the question." He tapped the paper. Gina wasn't answering any questions, not even something as tempting as "will you marry me?" until she had some answers to her own.

"You left, with all of your things. Why?"

"In case you said 'no,'" he explained. "I wanted to make a quick getaway if you said no and broke my heart. I humiliate easily."

"I don't understand."

"I left this beside you on the pillow." He started to smile. "You left the room in such a mess that you never even saw it, did you?"

"No," Gina admitted, remembering the rumpled bed and her quick exit. She looked down at the drawing again. "This isn't a joke?"

"I wouldn't joke about spending the rest of our lives together. From the first moment I saw you again I've been trying to figure out how to stay. So," he said, plucking the paper out of her hands so she would look at him. "Are you going to say 'yes'?" He paused, taking her into his arms. "Keep in mind that I've talked to a real estate agent, called my newspaper, and told them both that I intend to move back to Tyler and pick up after you 'til death do us part."

"You do?"

"Unless you say no, and in that case I'll go back to Chicago and be too sad to be funny any more and my career will come to a screeching halt."

"I thought you were going to ruin my weekend," she whispered, right before he kissed her.

"Is that a yes?"

"Absolutely," Gina declared, looping her arms around his neck. He looked relieved and surprised and very, very pleased with the world, which made her kiss him again.

"Let's go back to the inn for the rest of the weekend." He reached for her suitcase without letting her out of his embrace. "It's not Valentine's Day yet and I want to wake up with you tomorrow."

"Not too early?" she teased.

"I'll bring you breakfast in bed," Kurt promised.

"Which is only fair," she said, letting him lead her through the doorway, "since Eden said you were my Valentine's present."

"I'll have to thank her," Kurt said, tugging her closer. "But not yet. Let's let my mother and Eden wonder about us for a little while longer."

"We'll send flowers to both of them," Gina told him as she went into his arms for one more kiss. "Tomorrow."

BEHIND CLOSED DOORS

Heather MacAllister

CHAPTER ONE

"LOOK AT THIS FACE! Now, how can you tell me that cheese is more popular than the sexiest man in America?" Delia Mayhew, Tyler's youngest, and—in her opinion—most progressive librarian, held up three magazines dealing with various aspects of the Wisconsin cheese industry and a copy of *American Woman* magazine, impressively dog-eared in spite of its protective plastic cover.

Elise Fairmont, head librarian, sighed, something she'd been doing a lot lately. "Delia, you keep the circulation records yourself. You know *Cheeze Pleeze* usually draws more readers than *American Woman*—"

"Not this month." Delia tapped the magazine. "I think it's a trend."

She knew darn good and well that the worn state of the February issue of *American Woman* was solely due to the cover shot of one Justin

Archer, millionaire businessman, who the magazine had proclaimed "The Sexiest Man in America."

Not even *Cheeze Pleeze*'s usual back page cheesecake shot of some Wisconsin coed had attracted as much attention as Justin Archer's photo. Why, Delia had had to remove the full-color, tear-out poster of him to make sure it wasn't damaged before the magazine could be archived. She'd pinned it to her office wall for safekeeping.

Maybe he was the sexiest man in America, and maybe he wasn't. Personally, Delia preferred dark hair and eyes to streaked blond hair and impossibly blue eyes—though the poster of Justin, a former competitive swimmer wearing a racer's tiny Speedo swimsuit as he coached a Special Olympics team, had just about changed her mind.

But that wasn't the point. The point was that thirty-one percent more women than usual had found an excuse to enter the Alberta Ingalls Memorial Library to judge Justin's worthiness for themselves. Some more than once. An additional plus was that these women had brought their children with them, which in turn had swelled the attendance at Delia's afternoon story times. Bringing more children and teenagers into the library was Delia's personal mission in life.

And as children's librarian, it was also her job, a job that might be in jeopardy if library usage continued to dwindle.

"Delia," Elise began, not unkindly, "I hate to dampen your enthusiasm, but I have to trim our periodical expenses by at least ten percent. More, if I can."

"Then drop one of the cheese magazines!" Delia flipped through *Cheeze Pleeze* to the inside back cover and pointedly showed Elise the picture of a smiling brunette wearing a bikini made of three strategically placed cheddar wheels. "Do we really need this magazine?"

"If we want to keep the male members of the city council dropping by once a month, we do."

And they did, because the city council set the annual library budget. Delia indicated the other two magazines. "Then what about dropping one of these?"

Elise's gaze flitted between the two. "They both have such marvelous recipes."

"So do the others!" Delia gathered a stack of homemaker and craft-type magazines. "All these magazines are too much alike. Stain removal tips, wreath patterns, do-it-yourself holiday decorations, and articles on how to reorganize a closet. And it's February, so they've all got chocolate cake recipes, romantic dinner tips, and patterns for heart-shaped lace potpourri pillows.'' She returned them to the rack. "I'll bet we could put these out again next year and nobody would notice as long as we got the month right.''

When Elise looked as though she might actually be considering doing just that, Delia plunged ahead. "*American Woman* is the only magazine with a different slant. It's trendy and sophisticated.''

Elise frowned. "It's too New Yorky.''

"It's *modern.* Like cable TV. It's what young people want to see and read about. If we don't reflect their world, then we're going to lose them.'' If they hadn't already.

"Tyler just isn't like that,'' Elise said softly, maybe even wistfully.

Delia knew exactly what Tyler, Wisconsin, was like. She'd lived her whole life in the small town. And when she'd gone away to school, she hadn't gone very far—just to Madison, barely an hour away.

But in her beloved books she'd traveled all over the world—past, present and future. She could do anything and be anyone she wanted to be—as soon as she got the nerve.

But getting up the nerve was *her* problem. The goal here was to attract the youth of Tyler to the library and encourage them to read. Computers weren't the same as books. The Internet wasn't the same. TV wasn't the same. Watching videos wasn't the same.

Nothing was the same as reading and Delia was bound and determined that the people of Tyler remembered that.

Even if she had to put up with cheesecake photos.

''Why don't you wait until after the Book Lovers' Day carnival before you make any decisions?'' she suggested now. ''I just know that when people see how wonderful the new reading area is, they'll come here all the time.''

They both looked toward the windowed corner Delia had commandeered. ''You've done a great job,'' Elise told her, which was generous of her since Delia knew she had reservations about the whole project.

Delia had copied the reading area idea from the megabookstore where she'd worked part-time while she was in college in Madison. It was inconceivable to her that the store—which presumably wanted to sell books—*encouraged* people to linger and read. People seemed to forget it was a bookstore and treated it like a library.

So why shouldn't the library act like a bookstore, if that's what people wanted? Delia had talked Marge Phelps, who owned Marge's Diner, into providing muffins and cookies and some of Britt Marshack's cheesecake danishes for people to buy. Marge had also lent the library a big coffee urn.

And here Delia had gambled with her tiny budget, ordering designer coffee, the same coffee people paid outrageous amounts for at the specialty coffee shops. Delia was only charging fifty cents a cup. She justified underwriting the cost hoping that mothers with children would be attracted by the atmosphere and reasonable price and take an afternoon break by bringing their children to story time. She was introducing the reading area this Monday, on Valentine's Day, which the library always declared Book Lovers' Day.

"I'll tell you what," Elise said. "If your carnival can get people back into the library, I'll not only keep *American Woman*, I'll let you choose two more magazines. How's that?"

"Great!" But what Elise hadn't said was that if Delia's plan didn't work...

Well, it was going to work and that was that.

"I saw the announcement about the carnival in the *Citizen*," Elise said as she began walking toward the reference desk.

Delia knew what was coming. "Yes! Wasn't it great of Rob to give us a half-page?"

"I should hope he would! He knows I always recommend his and Judy's mysteries at the regional librarians' meeting. The least he can do is spare a few inches in his newspaper."

"And you know what?" Delia babbled on hoping to divert Elise. "He'll send Gina Santori to cover the whole event and include plenty of pictures of the new reading area—"

"And the special surprise guest?"

Rats. "Well, of course." Glancing pointedly toward the giant book-shaped clock on the wall, Delia edged toward the children's section.

"And the special surprise guest would be...?"

"A surprise."

Elise leveled a look at her, a look that said the surprise guest better not be the mayor's second cousin Nehemiah "Bobo" Boleski. Bobo's claim to fame was that he'd played professional hockey for five weeks with the Wisconsin Razors. Very few young kids in Tyler hadn't already seen Bobo flip out his partial bridge to expose his four missing front teeth, because the dentists liked to invite him for Dental Health Week in the fall.

Delia smiled brightly.

"Maybe a few hints would get folks talking," Elise suggested.

"Good idea." Delia escaped into the children's section and took her deep-pocketed craft apron from its red hook. "I'll do that."

"Mmm," was all Elise said.

Okay, so Delia had Bobo for a backup in case she couldn't persuade someone more famous to come.

It wasn't like she hadn't been trying. She'd sent out letters, e-mails, faxes and phoned dozens of people who might know someone famous.

At first, she'd hoped to find a celebrity who was charmed by the hopeful audacity of a small-town librarian and moved to make a grand gesture.

Or a donation. She'd had no luck, but Delia still held out hope for a miracle—that's what it would take now—even as she felt guilty because she was leaving Bobo hanging.

And that wasn't fair. He was a nice guy. Valentine's Day was Monday. Today was Friday and it was nearly three o'clock. No more stalling. She'd call him after story time.

Delia went to the colorful cardboard box that served as a table and storage container for floor pillows and pulled them out, arranging the primary-colored squares, stars, crescent moons and circles on the floor. She positioned her rocking chair next to them and sat in it to wait. She'd found that the children would come if they saw her sitting there, rather than waiting in the area if they were early.

Delia always had a book she planned to read along with a couple of alternates in case she had a lot of very young or older children.

Today's book was *Cheeboo, the Kangaroo*, a current children's bestseller. She'd even tried to get the official giant Cheeboo to come for the

Book Lovers' celebration, but the publisher hadn't been willing to pay for a trip to a small town. So Delia requested use of a Cheeboo costume and glumly discovered that the rental fee and insurance was more than her yearly budget for story time supplies.

Okay, fine. Reaching into one of the pockets on her apron, she stroked the fuzzy gray fur of the small stuffed Cheeboo she'd bought with her own money. Children who were especially quiet would be allowed to hold Cheeboo.

Where was everyone? It was near three, according to the book clock. Delia looked through the window blinds to the gray day outside. The clouds looked heavy with snow, but no flakes had fallen yet. A threat of snow shouldn't be enough to keep people away, not at this point in the winter. At least the Estevez and the Atwood children should be there. Bless them, they rarely missed. Jeremy Kelsey and Sara Blake, too.

Delia was considering giving Kaity's Kids, the local day care, a call, when a man entered the library.

Normally, a man entering the library was no big deal.

Normally, the men didn't look like this one.

Delia blinked. Several times.

She didn't know if the man blinked or not because he was wearing sunglasses. In the library. In February. And he kept them on, sliding them down his nose just a fraction of an inch as he peered over the tops at the room.

He was all black-leather jacket, dark pressed jeans, and sun-kissed hair. This was no local. At thirty, Delia had not only memorized the available men of Tyler, she'd cataloged them—cross-referenced by family and occupation—and knew which ones were in circulation.

No, he wasn't from Tyler.

But so what?

Really, why was she so set on a Tyler man? Did she want to stay in Tyler for the rest of her life? Hadn't she always wanted to travel? To get out and see the world? Meet new people—okay, meet new men? What was she waiting for? The handsome prince or the white knight from the fairy tales she'd gobbled up when she was nine years old?

In fact, this man looked familiar, as though he'd modeled for a fairy-tale prince. Didn't they always have blond hair?

The man headed over to the periodicals section and stopped by the wooden racks that held the latest issues of regional and national newspapers.

Delia had to lean sideways to keep him in view. Her rocker wasn't meant to lean sideways and creaked in protest. She stood and pretended to rearrange the shelf of books closest to her, then stopped.

What was she doing? What were the chances that he would mysteriously be drawn to the children's section and see her? Delia would be willing to bet her entire budget that he was no father. Fathers didn't wear clothes like that. Those were cool clothes and expensive, as well, she surmised. They were the kind of cool clothes she saw the male models wear in *American Woman*.

Not even the third floor of Gates Department Store carried those kinds of clothes. These were too trendy. Gates went for fashionably classic and well made.

Delia straightened. The man was still staring at the rack. Several of the bars were bare and he clearly hadn't found whatever newspaper he was looking for.

Heart pounding, Delia left the safety of the waist-high, mazelike shelves in the children's section and walked clear across the library and past the atrium before the quiver in her knees became noticeable.

An improvement. When she last approached a man, she'd only managed a few steps.

Well, so? So what if her knees shook. That's what rolling stools were for. Delia detoured to the adult fiction section and snagged one of the stools the librarians used when they were shelving books and wheeled it toward periodicals.

The man was looking over the top of his sunglasses at yesterday's papers. Why didn't he take off his sunglasses? Delia noticed several people eyeing him curiously.

She was almost within hailing distance. Rolling her stool next to him, she asked, "May I help you find something?"

Startled, he jerked his head back and his sunglasses fell to the floor.

Great. Delia sighed inwardly, all hope of being thought a ravishing and witty potential date completely gone. Not that wearing the storytime apron was helping her case any. She should have removed it first, but it didn't matter now. Her first impression was in progress.

The man stooped to the carpeted floor and retrieved his sunglasses. As he stood, he prepared to put them back on, hesitated, then met her eyes.

Delia froze. Blue, blue eyes, blond hair, square jaw... She'd hallucinated Justin Archer, sexiest man in America.

She really needed to get out more.

On the other hand, if she were going to hallucinate a man, Justin Archer was the one to hallucinate. It could have been Bobo Boleski.

Without his partial in.

"I didn't mean to startle you," she said, surprised she could speak.

"Not a problem." His lips curved in a small sexy half smile that hooked itself right into her heart. "I've been a little jumpy lately."

"Did you need help finding a newspaper?" Delia didn't blink as she spoke. If she blinked, the gorgeous apparition would waver and fade away.

The wariness left his eyes. "I was looking for the *Wall Street Journal.*"

She blinked. He was still there. "I know we subscribe to it." It was important to let him know Tyler wasn't a hopeless hick town.

"I've found that most libraries do." His easy smile prompted an answering one from her.

"You visit a lot of libraries?"

"Yeah. It's a hobby of mine."

Delia had never heard of a library hobby before and was about to ask him about it, when a flash of red caught her eye. The Kaity's Kids Day Care van had arrived and Kaity, in her bright red parka, was leading a group of children through the double glass doors to the coat room.

Delia had about three extra minutes. "Look, someone has probably left the paper in another part of the library. I'll go find it for you."

"Oh, don't go to the trouble."

"It's no trouble, really!" She heard her voice, girlish and eager, and cringed. "It's my job." Delia left him standing there.

Actually, it wasn't her job. Her job was story time, but there weren't any little bodies rolling on the pillows yet and she would be expected to help a library patron in need.

Delia found the newspaper in a heap on the floor by one of the computers. She picked it up, smoothed and folded it, then returned to the periodical section.

Justin Archer—or whoever he was—was gone.

CHAPTER TWO

DELIA WAS HELPLESS to stop her little whimper of disappointment. She ran through the metal security arch and double glass doors into the lobby.

He was nowhere in sight.

Had she only imagined him?

No, not the man—but his extreme likeness to Justin Archer, maybe. Probably. More than likely. Really—Justin Archer in Tyler, Wisconsin? She'd been staring at his poster too long.

As she stood there, more of her story-time regulars and their mothers arrived at the library.

"Miss Delia, Miss Delia!" Giggling, Sara Blake ran and hugged Delia's knees. "Did we miss our story?"

Delia smiled down at little girl with the blond hair and huge blue eyes. She was a charmer. "I'm just about to start."

"All right!"

As she bent to return the little girl's hug, Delia saw more children coming in through the glass doors. And behind them, she saw a car leaving the parking lot. The driver wore sunglasses. Maybe.

"Did you see a tall man—blond hair, sunglasses—leaving just now?" she asked Sara's mother, Molly. As the new owner of the Breakfast Inn Bed B&B, Molly was in a good position to know of any strangers in town.

Molly followed Delia's gaze. "No, I didn't. Why?"

The last of Delia's faint hope for a miracle faded away. "He was looking for the *Wall Street Journal* and I just found it. I guess he got tired of waiting."

They walked back into the main part of the library and Delia made it to the children's section in time to earn a reproving look from Elise just as Kaity's charges boiled out of the coat room and dived into the pillows with noisy shrieks and giggles.

"Hello boys and girls." Delia slipped onto her rocker and pulled the stuffed animal out of her pocket. "Who can tell who this is?"

"Cheeboo!" they shouted and flopped onto the pillows.

Delia held two fingers to her lips. "Let's use our indoor voices. Now, who is this?"

"It's Cheeboo!" several children said in loud stage whispers.

Delia didn't expect whispering, which was a good thing because she knew it wouldn't last.

"I wanna hold him!" cried Sara Blake, who knew the routine.

"The best listeners can hold Cheeboo while I read," Delia told them. "He's ready for his nap." *As are some of you,* she thought.

They all stilled and Delia gave Cheeboo to a quiet little girl on the fringes of the group. She was new and shy and was one child Delia actually hoped would become a bit noisier when she made friends. As she'd anticipated, the girl was immediately—but quietly—surrounded by Sara and some of the others who wanted a turn at holding the stuffed kangaroo next. Smiling to herself, Delia began reading the latest Cheeboo adventure.

In this story, Cheeboo was too lazy to leave his mother's pouch. He was comfortable and happy, but his mother wanted him to go out into the big world.

Delia knew just how he felt. The Tyler library was her kangaroo's pouch and she'd become too comfortable here.

There was a whole world waiting to be explored and Delia had read and dreamed about a life outside Tyler, Wisconsin for years. But the truth was, her two years attending school in Madison had taught her that she just wasn't a life-outside-of-Tyler sort of person. She was happy here and she adored her job. It was just that sometimes, like when she'd come face-to-face with the Justin Archer look-alike, Delia wondered if she'd look back on her life and have regrets.

Cheeboo sighed and Delia sighed right along with him.

After story time, she went into her office and called Bobo Boleski to confirm his appearance at the Book Lovers' Day carnival and regretfully decline his offer to man a kissing booth.

When she'd been speaking with Bobo, Delia had swiveled in her chair so she was facing the doorway, her back to the wall with the poster of

Justin Archer. Now, she could feel him staring at her.

Hanging up the telephone, she turned and faced the poster, inhaling sharply when she took a good look at the man's face.

The same blue eyes. The same jaw, the same hair... But what clinched it was the faintly self-deprecating half smile. She'd seen that same smile—in person. She knew it.

Delia went all cold and hot at the same time. Justin Archer, himself, had been in the Tyler library. Who knew why or how, but Delia knew with goose bump certainty that she'd seen and spoken to Justin Archer.

And she wanted to again. About being the celebrity guest at the Book Lovers' Day carnival, of course. He'd said libraries were a hobby and since he was here and all...

Delia closed her eyes and tried breathing deeply. She had to find him. There just wasn't time to wait and hope he paid another visit to the library.

Knees shaking, Delia left her office and found Pauline Martin, one of the aids. She was pushing an empty book cart from the adult fiction section.

Delia intercepted her. "Pauline, did you happen to see the man who was in here earlier? He was wearing sunglasses... Did he look familiar to you?"

"You mean that new high school basketball coach who's got all the teachers in a twitter?" Pauline asked.

Delia could believe the twitter part. "I don't think he was the coach." She'd only seen a black-and-white newspaper photo of the coach and he hadn't resembled Justin Archer in the slightest.

"Then I didn't see him," Pauline said. "Are you looking for something to do?" Pauline's eyes twinkled.

Delia smiled, remembering the question from years past. Pauline was a plump woman in her fifties who'd been a full-time library aid for years. As a child, Delia had spent hours helping her shelve books.

She shook her head. "I'm working on the carnival."

"Is Bobo coming?"

"Well, uh, yes...."

"Thought so." Nodding to herself Pauline

pushed the empty cart next to the stack of books waiting to be reshelved and started loading them.

"But he's not the surprise guest," Delia said rashly.

Pauline straightened, her mouth forming an "O." "Never say! Who is it?"

Delia swallowed. "A surprise."

"Oh, Delia, tell me! I work here!"

"You'll have to wait until Monday, just like everyone else." *And me, too.*

Pauline's expression turned speculative. "Now who could it be?" she murmured thoughtfully as she continued to load the cart. "I'll bet that's who Molly's got staying at her B&B. Quinn was in here this morning and said that Molly got a reservation from somebody who was real interested in privacy. He says Molly won't even tell him who it is. Am I right? Is that your surprise guest?"

"Could be," Delia said airily. She knew Pauline would probably go home tonight and discuss the possibilities with her friends. And that's what Delia wanted—people excited and talking about the carnival and then there'd be a whole crowd at the library on Monday.

Now all she had to do was track down Justin

Archer and convince him to come. Turning on her heel, she went to find Elise.

Elise was helping some high school students in the reference section.

"Elise," Delia whispered, more because she didn't trust her voice than because whispering was a library rule.

Elise finished up with the student she'd been helping and gestured to Delia.

Delia gestured back. She didn't want anyone to overhear them.

Brow creased, Elise stepped to the far side of the circular island. "What is it?"

"Did you see the man I was helping earlier?"

Elise shook her head.

"Sure you did," Delia insisted impatiently. "He was tall with blond hair—and he wore his sunglasses."

"Oh, that one." The older woman's voice sounded dismissive and she moved back toward her station to access the interlibrary loan program.

Delia drew a deep breath. "That was Justin Archer."

Elise didn't even look up. "The new coach at the high school?"

Delia just stopped herself from rolling her eyes. "No. *Justin Archer*. The guy on the cover of *American Woman*."

"Really? He told you he was Justin Archer?"

"Not exactly, but he looked just like him."

"Well, I suppose it could have been," Elise agreed to Delia's total shock. "That big computer expo was in Madison this week. Bigwigs came in from everywhere."

Delia knew that Justin had made his fortune in computers, but she was surprised Elise remembered.

Elise went on, oblivious to the fact that Delia was nearly hyperventilating. "The business teachers from the high school have all gone. That's why the computer classes are meeting in here to work on their winter research papers."

"So, so, you mean—so Justin Archer could have actually, really been here? In our library?"

At that, Elise looked up at her. "Isn't that what you said?"

She was acting like an adolescent girl in the throes of her first crush. Delia tried to collect herself. "Yes, yes, I did. He wanted to read the *Wall Street Journal*." She smacked her hand against her forehead. "Of course he wanted to read the *Wall Street Journal!* He's Justin Archer!''

She untied her apron and ran toward her office for her coat.

''Where are you going?'' Elise called after her.

''To find him!''

ALL JUSTIN WANTED was a copy of the *Wall Street Journal* before he checked into the B&B. Sure, he could access it online, but he spent enough time in front of a computer during the day.

The library had seemed like a good bet until all those women had started coming in. With his face plastered all over *American Woman,* one of them was bound to recognize him and cause a scene.

He sighed as he drove around the town square and risked pulling into a parking space in front of the drugstore on the opposite side of the square from the library.

Justin's life this past month had not been easy. When he'd first been notified that *American Woman*—a magazine he'd never heard of before—had selected him as their ''Sexiest Man in

America,'' he'd been mildly amused and flattered. He'd agreed to the story and to pose for the cover photos just to tweak his friends. He never thought anyone would take it seriously.

Beth had taken it seriously. Beth had taken it seriously when they'd been out on dates and other women had begun approaching him for autographs.

He wasn't always asked to sign paper, either.

What Justin couldn't figure out was that he was the same person he'd always been but people were just plain acting goofy around him. The cover of the magazine had been only the beginning. The press kept calling for interviews. Did they care about the next-generation video card Archer Computers was developing? No. They were on a ''bachelor watch,'' keeping tabs on whether or not Justin was still an eligible bachelor.

And Beth was doing her best to take him off the market. She'd become jealous and possessive—had she ever become possessive.

All the attention from the press wasn't helping. They'd even taken the Archer Computers logo—a man shooting a bow and arrow—and had turned it into a Cupid.

Monday was Valentine's Day, and back home in San Francisco, there was going to be an article in the Sunday paper about what the world's sexiest man was going to be doing to celebrate in the world's most romantic city.

Justin parked the car and rubbed his temples. What a nightmare. He knew Beth expected an engagement ring.

Even his parents expected an announcement. His mother had been quoted as saying that she was "more than ready for grandchildren."

On Tuesday, when Justin emerged from his town house, two photographers had snapped his picture, apparently considering themselves on some kind of celebrity stakeout. They'd struck again at lunch and had interrupted a delicate negotiation with a potential client.

And that was enough for Justin. Two hours later, he was on a plane for the Midwest Computer Expo in Madison, Wisconsin. It was a great excuse, if he did say so himself. He was away from the press, his parents—and Beth.

He wasn't in love with Beth and, once the next month's issue of the magazine was on the stands and the press left him alone, he hoped that she would realize that she wasn't in love with him, either.

Landing Justin Archer had become a matter of pride to her. With dozens of women pestering his secretaries and filling up his voice mail with suggestive messages—and if he *ever* discovered who had given out his unlisted home number, they were toast—he could see her point.

He was in a hideous position, and looking back, he could see how he was partly to blame. At the very beginning, when *American Woman* had announced their selection, Justin had maintained that he already had a girlfriend. He used it as a polite excuse to refuse dates, only somewhere along the line, girlfriend had become Girlfriend and now, Girlfriend expected to become fiancée.

Justin didn't know whether it was better to just get her a ring and break the engagement later, or continue to ignore everyone's expectations. Either way, Beth would get hurt.

Justin groaned aloud. He'd been sitting in the car for so long, the windows were fogging. Buttoning his inadequate leather jacket, he emerged from the rental car and cautiously approached the drugstore, hoping they had a newsstand inside.

They did, but there weren't any copies of the paper—or *American Woman* he was gratified to see. He bought a copy of the *Tyler Citizen,* the local paper, and returned to his car.

This morning the press had discovered him and Justin was on the run again. He'd found a brochure for the Breakfast Inn Bed in his hotel lobby. Advertised as a "romantic hideaway," Justin wasn't attracted so much by the romance aspect, as by the hideaway part. It promised complete privacy in a small town, and he planned to hold them to it—if he got there without anyone recognizing him.

He'd had a few anxious minutes at the library, but the fresh-faced girl who'd approached him didn't seem to know who he was.

He took the glossy brochure and studied the tiny line drawing of a map on the reverse side. He was on Main Street, and according to the map, all he had to do was take Main to Ivy and he'd be there.

The Breakfast Inn Bed turned out to be better than he'd expected. It looked brand new, but must have been a recently restored Victorian. He could practically smell the fresh paint.

Justin parked his car, removed his carry-on and slung his garment bag over his shoulder. So far, so good. No one around. If he could just check in and get to his room undetected by the other guests, stoke up that wood-burning stove and then veg out with a book and bottle of something. He had bought several somethings from which to choose. Maybe tonight he'd break out a fine old brandy, the sort that went with wood-burning stoves and techno thrillers.

Justin stepped into a spacious entry and found a small desk by the polished wooden staircase. No one was there and he hesitated to break the quiet by calling out. He was trying to decide what to do, when a petite blond woman rushed in from outside, pulling off her gloves as she hurried to the desk.

"Hi, I'm Molly Spencer, the owner of Breakfast Inn Bed." She stuck out a hand warm from her gloves. He hadn't thought to bring gloves. "You must be Richard Longfield."

Justin drew a deep breath. His successful escape depended on whether this woman was discreet or not. "As you'll see by my credit card,

I'm not Richard Longfield, but that's the name I'll be using this weekend. As we discussed when I made the reservation, I don't want anyone to know I'm here. *Anyone*," he emphasized.

"Certainly."

At her wary expression, he explained, "If I don't get some downtime, I'll go nuts."

At that, she grinned and turned the registry toward him. "Gotcha."

Justin signed the fake name, though why she had him do so, he didn't know.

"Sorry I wasn't here when you arrived," she apologized as he took out his wallet. "I took my daughter to story time at the library and was running a little behind schedule. It looks like it might snow and I wanted to be sure we had plenty of supplies for breakfast."

Here was the moment of truth. Justin handed her his card and watched for any sign of recognition.

She stared at the name, then shook her head slightly as she made an impression of the card. "Are you on television?" she whispered. "I don't watch much TV."

"I'm not usually on television, but I have been a couple of times lately." He was *not* going to tell her he was supposedly the sexiest man in America.

But Molly Spencer was a true professional. She merely nodded and returned his card. "I've put you in the Bachelor's Puzzle."

"I'm already in a bachelor's puzzle," Justin murmured.

Molly laughed. "Each room is named after the pattern of the quilt that's on the bed." She came out from behind the desk. "Yours is the Bachelor's Puzzle." Gesturing for him to follow her, she indicated a living area off to the right. "If you decide you miss company, most of the guests gather in here before returning to their rooms in the evening."

Justin, wary of encountering other guests, stuck his head in the room long enough to take in a fireplace and some comfortable-looking chairs and sofas.

"The door on the far side leads to a small library and game room."

"A library?" Justin brightened. "Now that I'll have to visit." Probably in the middle of the night, though he didn't mention it.

"You can eat breakfast in the dining room, straight through there—" Molly nodded to a formally decorated room "—but I imagine you'd like our trademark breakfast in bed."

"You got that right."

Molly smiled, then Justin noticed her glancing over his shoulder before ushering him toward the stairs. "Go on up and wait for me." A moment later, he heard voices and appreciated Molly's understanding.

The front door opened and he heard Molly greet a man and a woman, offering them tea in the living room by the fire.

Hot tea sounded surprisingly good to Justin. Surprising, since he didn't think he'd ever had afternoon tea in his life. Of course, he hadn't been this chilled in awhile, either.

"We're completely booked because of the holiday this weekend," Molly said when she joined him on the landing. She unlocked the door to a room at the end of the hall, which pleased him.

He was even more pleased when he saw the king-size brass bed and the wood-burning stove he'd been looking forward to.

"And here's the Bachelor's Puzzle quilt."

The quilt was made of squares and rectangles that fit together like a puzzle, if Justin used his imagination. It wasn't a frilly pattern, which was a relief, but that was the only bachelor thing about it. He murmured politely and could tell from Molly's expression that he wasn't fooling her. He could also tell that she didn't mind.

"Would you like me to bring you some tea and cookies?" Molly offered. "I don't usually, but you look like you could use a cookie."

Justin set his bags on the folding luggage stand and smiled his first truly relaxed smile in weeks. "That would be great. Thanks."

"No problem." She let herself out of the room.

Justin sat on the bed, then dropped back onto the pillows. The stress of the last weeks drained away. He exhaled. He was hiding out in the middle of a small town where people didn't seem to have heard of Justin Archer.

Minutes later, there was a knock on the door and Molly brought him a pot of tea with warm chocolate chip cookies.

Yes, this place would do nicely.

He might never leave.

CHAPTER THREE

DELIA HAD ONLY A vague idea about where to find Justin Archer and an even vaguer idea about what to say to him when she did. That she might not find him at all was simply not an option.

She was prepared to drive all the way to the computer expo in Madison if she had to, but first, she stopped by the drugstore newsstand. Maybe he'd gone there to buy a copy of the paper he wanted.

She was in luck. The clerk, a young high school girl, remembered him and he had, indeed, bought a newspaper—the *Citizen*. That part didn't fit. Why would he bother to buy a copy of the local paper? But the leather jacket and sunglasses did.

"Those were the coolest shades," the girl told Delia. "They cost, like, three hundred fifty dollars. I never saw an actual person who wore them before. Is he a friend of yours?"

I wish. "No. Just someone who came into the library this afternoon."

"The *library?*" The girl's face underwent a transformation as she obviously reconsidered the coolness factor of the library. "Whoa."

And *that* was exactly the reaction Delia wanted. "Yeah. The library's a happenin' place," she said, wondering if she'd used current youth slang, or not. "Come and check us out."

"Check Us Out" had been last year's slogan. The play on words went right over the clerk's head. She was busy with another customer anyway.

Delia thanked her and left.

Now what?

He'd bought a newspaper and it was almost dinnertime. Could he possibly have gone to get something to eat? He wouldn't have bought a newspaper if he was just going to turn around and drive back to Madison, would he? At least not a local paper.

Proud of her newly discovered detective skills, Delia headed for Marge's Diner, just off the town square.

As always, warm air scented with coffee and whatever wonderful and calorie-laden goodie

Marge had just taken from the oven whooshed over Delia when she opened the door. Her stomach rumbled in automatic response.

But a quick glance toward the counter revealed that all the red vinyl seats were occupied by local people.

When she checked the booths, Delia's heart gave a thump as she saw Caroline, who was new in town, serving coffee to a customer who was hidden by an open newspaper.

Delia forced herself to walk toward the back, annoyed with herself because her heart was thumping. So she was going to approach an attractive stranger. Big deal. What was the worst that could happen?

Delia had an active imagination, and it helpfully supplied her with a dozen scenarios incorporating various degrees of humiliation. Fortunately, nothing happened. Nothing happened because Delia belatedly realized that the hand accepting the cup of coffee wore rings and nail polish.

She sighed. So much for her detective skills. Waving goodbye to Marge behind the counter, Delia started for the door.

"Hear you've got some big shot comin' in for your carnival," Marge called out to her.

Everyone at the counter turned to look at Delia.

"Pauline was just in here," Marge went on. "She says you've got him stashed over at the Breakfast Inn Bed."

"No. Not at the Breakfast Inn Bed."

"So you *do* have somebody big coming in."

Delia had a choice. She could squash the rumor right now and send her hopes for a spectacular attendance right down the drain, which would be the safe thing to do.

But she'd played it safe her whole life and right now, the library didn't need safe. *She* didn't need safe.

"Of course!" she promised rashly.

"Who is it?" This came from a young woman Delia had never seen in the library before.

"A surprise," Delia answered. "In fact, we've got lots of surprises for the carnival and I expect to see everybody there!"

With that, she escaped from the homey warmth of the diner and emerged onto the darkening street, swallowing the sick feeling that had invaded her stomach.

Being unsafe wasn't all it was cracked up to be. Now, what was she going to do? This situation was her own fault and she knew it. She should never have led Pauline on. The rumor was taking on a life of its own and now the Breakfast Inn Bed was involved. *A guest who's real interested in privacy...*

Delia's knees started quivering again. Justin Archer. It had to be.

It had better be.

As she pulled into the driveway of the Breakfast Inn Bed, Delia wished she'd paid more attention to the car that had driven away from the library. There was nothing special about it, just as there was nothing special about any of the cars in the parking area reserved for the B&B guests. Still, there were cars there, so that was hopeful.

Delia walked inside, and as usual, was overwhelmed by an urge to repeatedly wipe her feet on the welcome mat.

The place was all elegance and polished wood. Gentle conversational murmurs came from the large living room in front of her as Quinn and Molly's guests gathered by a fire. It looked like something out of a magazine.

As Delia admired the scene, Molly, carrying a tray with used tea things on it, carefully came down the stairs.

"Delia!" she exclaimed when she saw her. "Did Sara leave her Barbie doll at the library again?"

"Not this time." At Molly's nod, Delia followed her through a formal dining room, through a swinging door into the kitchen.

"What's up?" she asked, turning off the range under a pot of water that had just begun to boil.

"Do you remember me asking you about the man who wanted the *Wall Street Journal* at the library?"

Molly furrowed her brow as she poured a small amount of boiling water into a china teapot, swished it around and emptied it before adding loose tea leaves. "Vaguely."

"Tall, good-looking." *Incredibly good-looking.* "Well dressed...expensive sunglasses...?"

Though she said nothing, Delia got the idea Molly knew exactly who she was talking about. She decided to go for it. "I wondered if he might be staying here."

Molly quickly glanced at her before concentrating on pouring the boiling water into the pot. "I have a lot of guests staying here this weekend. We're fully booked."

"Yes, but is he one of them?"

Molly gave her a sharp look, then softened it by handing Delia one of the cookies she'd arranged on a plate. "My guests value their privacy," was all she said before spooning jam into a small china dish.

But that was enough for Delia. Usually, Molly was very chatty.

"Delia, would you look in the pantry and see if I've got any more strawberry preserves?"

A change of subject. Interesting—and encouraging. Delia nodded and popped the rest of the chocolate chip cookie into her mouth. Molly's pantry was practically as big as the kitchen in the tiny apartment Delia used to live in.

She'd hated living alone, and besides, if she was going to pay rent, she'd rather pay her parents, and so had moved back home. "I don't see any."

The phone rang just then. "Would you be a sweetie and go down into the basement for a couple of jars?" Molly asked as she reached for the telephone. "And remember the door sticks, so keep it propped. If it shuts, just pound the spot above the knob and it'll open."

Delia stepped over a heavy decorative iron with a calico bow and felt into the darkness for the light switch. She stepped down a couple of steps before finding it and when she turned it on, was blasted by the light from a low-hanging bulb. Someone had once knotted the cord, but it had slipped and was now about level with Delia's forehead. She ducked under it and went in search of Molly's homemade preserves.

Molly had everything labeled and organized, so Delia found them right away and climbed the stairs, pushing against the heavy door which had drifted shut except for the iron prop.

"Here you go." She set the jars on the counter.

"Thanks." Molly was refilling the milk pitcher.

"Molly, if the blond man with the sunglasses were staying here, would you tell me?"

"No."

"If he *weren't* staying here, would you tell me?"

Molly gave her an exasperated look. "No."

"Why not? If he's not staying here, then it wouldn't matter what you told me."

Molly opened and closed her mouth. "Oh, go shelve some books!" She picked up the tray and walked out of the kitchen.

"Yes!" Delia allowed herself a short victory celebration. She'd done it. She'd found Justin Archer! Now all she had to do was convince him to come to the Book Lovers' Day carnival.

She went charging after Molly, stopping at the entrance to the living room, but prepared to go in if she saw Justin Archer sitting by the fire. He wasn't, of course. That would have been too easy.

"No," Molly said when she came out into the foyer.

"You don't even know what I'm going to ask."

"So ask."

"I want to talk with him—"

"No."

"Will you at least tell him I want to talk with him?"

"No."

"*Molly!*"

"Delia, the man wants privacy and as long as he's staying here, that's what he's going to get."

"It's Justin Archer, isn't it?"

Molly leveled a look at her. "There is no Justin Archer registered here," she said evenly.

"Oh." Delia hadn't been expecting that. She'd been so certain... "Well, okay, if he isn't Justin Archer, he looks enough like him to pretend to be him and that's good enough for me."

"Delia!"

"Please, Molly. I've got to come up with someone for the carnival on Monday and I've only got Bobo confirmed and people are expecting somebody big and the future of the library depends on it—please!"

Molly wavered, but stood firm. "I'm sorry, Delia. I can't." With a regretful smile, she headed back to the kitchen.

Delia suddenly felt very tired. There had to be a way to contact Justin Archer. There *had* to be.

She just couldn't think of one right now. As she rebuttoned her coat her gaze fell on the reception desk and the guest book. Before she chickened out, she ran over to it and looked at the latest entries.

Couples and one single male name. Richard

Longfield, appropriately in the Bachelor's Puzzle room. Taking a chance, Delia went behind the desk, got a piece of the Breakfast Inn Bed stationery and hastily wrote a note inviting Mr. Longfield to the Book Lovers' Day carnival. Then she added her name and phone number with a request that he contact her if he planned to attend.

Sealing the envelope, Delia put it in the wooden mailbox marked Bachelor's Puzzle.

While she was at it, she wrote out shorter invitations for the other rooms and put those in their boxes so Molly wouldn't get suspicious over the Bachelor's Puzzle one.

Feeling pleased with herself, Delia left, ready to spend the evening by her phone.

JUSTIN STOOD BY THE window in his bedroom and finished his third cup of most excellent coffee. He was filled with a sense of peace and well-being, not to mention caffeine.

He set the delicate china cup back in its saucer. When was the last time he'd indulged himself by staying up most of the night reading?

And then to wake up to the breakfast to end all breakfasts. Well, life didn't get much better.

In fact, he wanted to do it all over again today. And he planned to.

He'd been watching the other guests leave from his window and figured most of them were gone, or at least enough of them had left so that he could chance leaving his room to find another book to read.

Justin picked up his breakfast tray, thinking he'd save Molly a trip up the stairs to get it.

The foyer was deserted except for a little girl who sat at the reception desk and industriously traced giant-sized numbers over and over.

"May I help you?" she asked in a voice that made him smile.

"I was on my way to the kitchen. Can you show me where it is?"

"Yes. My name is Sara and I live here, so I know where it is." She slid off her chair and led him through the dining room.

They found Molly and a man about his own age working in the kitchen.

"More dishes, Mommy!" Sara announced.

Molly looked up and smiled at him. "Thanks! But you didn't have to bring them down."

She was rolling dough balls and setting them on a cookie sheet. All right, more chocolate chip cookies, Justin thought. He might not ever leave this place. "No problem. I wanted to get a book."

"Here I'll take that." The man reached for the tray. "I'm Quinn Spencer. We're glad to have you staying with us." Outwardly, he gave Justin an easy smile, but his gaze held a territorial warning.

It was a look with which Justin was becoming very familiar. Would the effects from that damn magazine never end?

"He's my new daddy," Sara told him and hugged Quinn's leg. He set the tray by the sink, reached down and picked her up, the very picture of domestic bliss.

Message received, not that the guy had any worries from him. "Congratulations," Justin said.

"Thank you." Molly beamed.

It was all getting a little too sugary for him. "Is the library through the living room?"

"Yes, or this door takes you directly into it," Molly confirmed with a gesture to the door on the other side of the center island where she was working.

Justin hoped the library wasn't just a couple

of shelves stuck in a corner and it wasn't. This was an honest-to-gosh old-fashioned library with floor-to-ceiling shelves and great leather chairs. Justin inhaled, imagining a whiff of ancient cigar smoke with the leather and old paper smell.

For now, he bypassed the modern books, easily identified by their garish jackets and headed for the genuine leather-bound volumes. Who knew what treasures he'd find there? He moved the library ladder over to the far corner, his eye on some books that looked as though they hadn't been handled in decades, and soon lost track of the time.

CHAPTER FOUR

SATURDAY MORNING DAWNED and Delia realized she'd irritated her family by keeping them off the phone for nothing. He hadn't called.

This time, Delia was ready with a Plan B. She was going to rotate the books in Molly's library. Molly and the library had an arrangement where they shared books, particularly the popular new bestsellers. Delia was in charge of trading out the volumes and that's what she was going to do today.

If, during the course of her duties, she managed to run into Justin or Richard or anybody faintly interesting, then so much the better.

It was nearly ten o'clock by the time Delia loaded the box of books into her little hatchback and drove over to the B&B. She was running just the slightest bit behind because she hadn't been able to decide what to wear. Everything in her closet looked too librarianish, but since this was her Saturday to work, she really had no choice but to look librarianish. At last deciding on a soft wool jumper in a light green plaid that Elise once told her made her eyes sparkle, she slipped on a pair of dressy flats instead of her usual tennis shoes. She took the time to put hot rollers in her dark hair, wishing she had the courage to make it blond hair. It had been a while since she'd worked with hot rollers and the results were bouncy and full of static electricity.

So, after spending way too much time fussing with her hair, she went outside and it got all windblown anyway. Now she remembered why she usually wore it pulled back.

Delia's first clue that something was going on at the B&B was the fact that the graveled area used for parking was full and she had to park on the street halfway down the block. First though, she pulled into the driveway behind another car and unloaded her box of books so she wouldn't have to carry them as far.

Her second clue was walking into a foyer crowded with women. Quinn and Molly Spencer guarded the staircase. From far above Sara, eyes wide, looked down on them.

"There's Delia!" someone called.

Delia had just taken in Molly's accusing look when the group turned to her and she came face to face with Pauline, who had this Saturday off from the library. "Elise said—oh, Delia, it's Justin Archer, isn't it? He's the surprise guest!" Her excitement was mirrored on the faces of the other women.

Delia had wanted people excited, but this was out of control. "Pauline, I never said Justin Archer was staying here! I didn't," she repeated loudly so Molly could hear. Molly heard, but obviously didn't believe her. "*You* were the one who said Quinn mentioned—"

"But you saw him in the library." Pauline's voice rang out clearly.

"That was the library. That wasn't here," Delia corrected without thinking. She'd been so concerned about turning the attention away from Breakfast Inn Bed that she hadn't realized how her words would be interpreted.

"There!" Pauline turned to the crowd in triumph. "I told you he was in Tyler!"

"But—"

Delia's protest was drowned out by someone shouting, "Molly, ask him to come down!"

Molly looked near to tears and Quinn threw a protective arm around her. "Ladies, you'd better leave now."

"We just want to welcome him to Tyler..."

"I'm having a little dinner party and wondered... "

"The Tyler chamber of commerce is having a special Sunday afternoon..."

"My daughter..."

Delia edged toward the living room and slipped inside so she could think. She had to get to Justin Archer before those women did—if they hadn't already scared him off by now.

"Ladies, please! We're just trying to run a bed and breakfast!" Quinn pleaded.

"Delia would know his schedule," she heard someone say. "She's in charge of the carnival."

At the sound of her name, Delia froze, then hurried through the living room toward the library. It was one thing to hint that someone important was coming to Book Lovers' Day. It was another thing to flat out promise Justin Archer's presence—especially before she asked him. And she still intended to ask him, if she ever got the—

She stood in the doorway, the weight of the box of books she carried forgotten.

The morning sun gilded the blond head of a man sitting in a leather wing chair, his feet propped on an ottoman. She could only see part of his face, but it was enough.

She'd found Justin Archer.

Her mouth went dry. Here was her chance. The man was so absorbed in his book that he didn't know about the reception waiting for him in the foyer.

All Delia had to do was take the two steps into the room and talk to him. She even had a legitimate reason for being there.

So why wouldn't her feet move?

She remembered the way he looked in the library. She remembered his smile and the sound of his voice. And she remembered his poster on her office wall. She remembered his shoulders, his chest, his stomach...

He was more man than she'd ever dealt with in her life. She wasn't the sort of woman who knew how to wrap a man around her little finger and have him eager to do whatever she wanted. She'd say her little speech, which she hadn't made up yet, he'd listen with a polite smile on his face, then just as politely turn her down and go back to reading his book.

No, a man like Justin would need a unique approach, or an approach by a woman he'd find unique.

He turned the page of his book, his fingers reverently sliding down the yellowing paper as he gently smoothed the center.

Recognition hit Delia. A book lover. Justin Archer was a fellow book lover.

Delia felt her heart turn over. Whatever else he was faded into insignificance. Surely she could convince a book lover to help the library.

Think of something to say. Something unique and witty. But natural. It's got to sound natural. She'd better hurry. Any second and he'd sense he was being watched.

As Delia hesitated, she heard a loud commotion in the foyer. The women weren't storming the stairs, were they?

"Where's Delia?" she heard faintly.

Suddenly, she backed out of the library and set her books just outside the door before fleeing to the kitchen. Yes, she wanted to talk to Justin, but she didn't want to be interrupted and she certainly didn't want to lead those women right to him.

She'd just wait out here in the kitchen until Quinn and Molly convinced the women to go home.

"Delia?" Someone was coming.

Delia didn't want to talk to anyone, either. Quickly stepping over the iron, she entered the basement and hid there in the dark as someone hurried into the kitchen.

"Well, where is she?" The voice sounded a lot like Molly. Delia didn't want to talk with Molly just yet, either. Molly wasn't in a mood to listen to rational explanations.

"I don't know. One minute she was there and the next she wasn't."

The voices faded and Delia reached for the light switch. Why couldn't the builders have put it in a more convenient place? In the process of groping around, she banged her forehead into the lightbulb. She stopped the swinging cord and finally found the switch.

There was a burst of light and then instant blackness. Oh, wonderful. She'd popped the lightbulb.

It was probably best that she wait in the dark until things cooled down anyway.

Carefully feeling around her feet for any scurrying creatures, Delia sat on the steps and thought about how to approach Justin, assuming he'd still be here after this morning, which she doubted.

Delia could hear excited voices, but they seemed to be coming from different directions. What was going on now?

A moment later she heard running footsteps and the door to the basement was yanked open. A man was silhouetted in the light and in that instant of full illumination, Delia recognized Justin Archer.

She gasped, but before she could shout out a warning, Justin shoved the iron aside with his foot and slammed the door shut, his breathing loud in the dark.

Outside the door, Delia heard women's voices and was embarrassed for Tyler. A person would think they'd never had a celebrity stay in town before.

Maybe with good reason.

Justin hadn't moved from the top of the stairs as far as Delia could tell. She imagined that he was listening at the door. At some point, she was going to have to let him know that he wasn't alone, and let him know without startling him so that he lost his footing on the steep steps.

"But I swear he came in here!" The shrill voice sounded just outside the door and Delia winced.

"Well, he's gotta be somewhere!"

"Maybe he's hiding in the pantry."

Delia heard the door next to them open and a click as the light was switched on.

"Not here, darn it."

Even though she was in pitch black and Justin didn't know she was there, Delia felt her face grow hot with embarrassment. She couldn't believe that these women were hunting him down like some kind of animal.

Weren't you doing the same thing? a little voice asked.

But that was different, wasn't it? She had a good cause, didn't she?

It *was* different, right?

"What's this door?"

"The basement, I think."

"Try it."

Delia inhaled sharply as the knob turned and rattled, but the door didn't open.

"I think it's locked."

"Why would Molly lock her basement?"

"Well, you know, if I had all those strangers staying in my home, I'd lock my basement and a lot more besides."

To Delia's relief, the voices faded away and she released the breath she hadn't known she was holding.

There was a split second of silence and then, "Am I correct in assuming that I'm not alone in here?" asked a low male voice.

Oops. "That's right."

"Ah. Female."

"Right again." Would he recognize her voice?

There was a short silence. "I suppose you'd like to get out of the basement."

"Well...yes."

"Is there another door?"

"I don't think so."

"It figures. At the risk of unduly alarming you, would you mind waiting here for a few more minutes?"

"I don't think that sounds alarming at all. After listening to those women outside, I think it sounds very wise.''

"Reasonable *and* perceptive. A winning combination so far,'' he said.

If only all men were that easily impressed, Delia thought. She heard brushing sounds and guessed that he was looking for the light.

"The bulb is out,'' she told him.

"You were here in the dark?''

"I just blew it out. Watch for it. It hangs on a real low cord—''

A smacking sound told her Justin had unexpectedly located the lightbulb. ''You weren't kidding.''

Delia tried to imagine where it had hit on his body. It had bumped her right in the forehead, so if he was standing on the same step...maybe his chest. A tiny sigh escaped.

"What are you doing?'' she asked when she heard more noises.

"Tying it higher. It feels as though someone's already done that once before. There. That should hold.''

"Good. I wasn't looking forward to playing dodge the lightbulb anymore.''

She heard a sound that might have been a chuckle. "Is there another light down here?"

"Not that I know of."

"So we're destined to be strangers in the dark." The way he said it made their situation sound terribly romantic.

He must not have recognized her voice from yesterday, not that there was a reason he should have. "We'll have to think of a secret password so that we'll know each other when we meet again." Oh, how dumb. Delia couldn't believe she'd said that out loud. Like Justin Archer wasn't going to break the speed limit driving out of Tyler as soon as he got out of the basement.

"Plastics?"

"What?"

"The secret password. Plastics."

"Why plastics?"

"It was a joke. A line from some movie."

"Which one?"

"I don't remember. My parents say it all the time and laugh."

"Yeah, my parents say weird stuff like that, too."

"And some day we'll bug our kids." Delia heard the smile in his voice. "It'll all even out."

Our kids. Delia's breathing and heartbeat got out of sync at the thought of doing anything with Justin Archer that might result in children.

Talk about skipping a few crucial steps in the relationship. So far, they hadn't even exchanged names, so he didn't know who she was or what she looked like. Delia was thinking that wasn't such a bad thing at all, when Justin climbed to the top of the stairs.

"I don't hear anyone in the kitchen. Ready to make our escape?"

No. But she knew the question was rhetorical. She'd also decided that she wasn't going to bother him about the carnival—not after everything he'd been through today. The library was important, but not important enough to cause riots.

She sighed a little private goodbye then heard the repeated twisting of the doorknob.

"Damn. The door can't be locked—not from the inside. Doesn't that violate some sort of building code?"

Delia got as far as opening her mouth to tell him to pound the spot right above the doorknob until the turning mechanism fell back into place and then stopped.

She was alone in the dark with the sexiest man in America, and for all he knew, she was the sexiest woman in America.

Delia felt her romantic soul take flight. This was like a dream. Fate had given her a perfect opportunity. In fact, fate had done a bang-up job lately, first, incredibly sending Justin Archer not only to Tyler, but into the library itself, and, when Delia had failed to capitalize on that meeting, offering a second chance.

Fate would become justifiably cross if Delia didn't put forth a little effort on her own behalf.

This was her chance to become anyone she wanted. And why not? After all, it wasn't likely that she'd ever meet Justin Archer again. Men like Justin didn't notice the Delias of this world. Just look at what had happened yesterday. She'd made no more impression on him than a piece of furniture.

He pulled at the door a couple more times, then quit. "Looks like we're stuck until somebody comes looking for us again."

Delia thought it was nice of him to include her as someone who would be searched for. "Do you have to be somewhere?" If he did, then she'd try the door herself. But if he didn't...

"Nope. I'm on vacation," he said to her delighted relief. "How about you? What were you doing in the basement?"

She should have anticipated that question. "Molly keeps her preserves and pickles down here."

As she hoped, he assumed that's why she'd been in the basement.

"Hey, it's nice to know we won't starve before somebody finds us."

Delia laughed. He was taking this awfully well. "Molly will be in here either fixing lunch or tea. It shouldn't be too long."

"So where are you exactly?"

"I'm sitting about four steps below you."

"Like some company?"

"Sure." She wished her heart would stop pounding so hard at these moments.

Justin carefully picked his way down the stairs and she felt his weight on the wooden step where she was sitting. "I'm sitting on the next one down from you."

"Gotcha." He sat beside her.

The steps weren't all that wide and there was nothing but an open hand rail between them and the concrete floor. Very cozy.

"Have you got enough room?" he asked. "Don't let me push you too close to the edge."

"I'm fine."

"Just a second." His thigh pressed against hers as he reached across her and felt for the other side. "Okay. You've got a few spare inches." He settled back, but his thigh didn't.

Delia swallowed.

It was just a thigh, for pity's sake.

A hard thigh. Justin's thigh.

She inhaled a steadying breath and her nose was filled with the faint scent of his soap and shaving cream. This wasn't a "cologney" smell, identifiable at twenty paces. Delia was pretty good at recognizing all the popular brands because drenching themselves in cologne after gym class was a fad among the younger teen-aged boys who came into the library after school.

Justin's scent was subtle and refreshing. She inhaled again, unable to recall the last time she'd been close enough to a man to smell the soap he used. The dark must have heightened her senses.

"Are you sure you're okay?" His voice sounded slightly above her and to the left.

"Oh, yeah," she answered. "I'm just fine."

"I can hear you sniffing."

Delia bit her lip and willed herself to breathe normally.

"Are you crying?" he asked, resignation in his voice.

"No!"

"Are you about to cry?"

"Why would I be about to cry?"

"Maybe you're afraid of the dark. I don't know—women have been doing strange things around me lately."

"Crying isn't so strange."

"I've found that crying can be used as an extremely effective weapon."

"How very cynical."

"I have reason to be."

"Why?" Though she suspected she already knew the reason.

"Let's just say I've learned firsthand about crocodile tears."

"Maybe they were genuine tears."

"Not likely."

Delia found herself intensely curious about the woman who cried crocodile tears at Justin. Nothing in the article had mentioned a wife or girlfriend, but really, a man like Justin without a woman in his life? Impossible. "What did you do to her?"

"Why do you think I did something to her?"

"Why was she crying then?"

He made an exasperated sound. "You women always stick together, don't you?"

"And you men don't?"

He was silent. Delia resisted the urge to say something. They'd been volleying the conversational ball back and forth and it was his turn. It was a strange conversation and Delia had never participated in one like it before. They hadn't even exchanged names, which suited her just fine.

"You know," Justin said at last, "a few weeks ago, I would have said, 'yeah, guys stick together.' But I don't know anymore."

"What happened?"

He shifted. "I...won a type of award."

Delia knew exactly what he was talking about, but the fact that he hadn't gone into detail meant he didn't want her to know. "Congratulations," she said, not knowing what else to say.

"It's not a congratulations type of award."

Well, now he had to expect her to ask. "What kind of award is it then?"

"The truth is that it was just a publicity gimmick, but people are taking the thing seriously."

Neatly answered. Delia relaxed, feeling her muscles protest after being held stiffly against him. "And you don't take the award seriously."

"If I did, then I'd be a real jerk. I kind of feel like one now."

"Why?"

"I didn't pay enough attention to what would be expected of me. The magazine—the one that gives the award—offered to make a donation to my favorite charity, which happens to be the Special Olympics, and that's all I paid attention to."

"You don't sound like a jerk to me," Delia told him quietly.

"Yeah, well. People are getting hurt over this thing. Nice people—at least they used to be nice."

"Are they people who cry crocodile tears?"

He laughed. "You're good."

Delia absorbed his praise like a sponge in water. She'd managed to hold the interest of the sexiest man in America for several minutes.

And she wasn't ready to let go yet.

CHAPTER FIVE

"I'M NOT SO MUCH good as curious. You appear to lead an interesting life."

"It's not boring, I'll give it that."

"Not if hiding out in basements is part of it."

"No—that would be one of the unexpected perks I've been given lately."

Delia almost felt sorry for him. "So what is your life like when it isn't so...perky?"

"What do you mean?"

"Well...what do you do?" She knew he was the millionaire owner of Archer Computers, but she didn't know exactly what he did during the course of a typical day.

"Ah...let's don't go that route."

What was he talking about? "What route is that?"

"You know, the typical getting-to-know-you interview in which we define people by their jobs and occupations. I'd like to stay unde-fined."

"Why? Are you an ax-murderer, or something?"

"Not yet," he muttered. "Hey—kidding."

"I knew that."

"Actually, you didn't. You don't know anything about me."

Delia wasn't about to correct him. "I know that you don't have an ax with you."

"Good point." He shifted and Delia imagined him gesturing with his hands. "We're in a unique position. We don't know what the other looks like, except for the fact that I'm male and you're female, so we can relate on a different level without going through the typical social filters."

"Interesting theory." Except that she knew exactly what he looked like down to the tiny crescent-shaped scar that disappeared under his chin. But she could go with it.

"For instance," he continued, "tell me what you do during the day that doesn't have anything to do with your job."

Delia was silent. What was there about her that could possibly interest him? She lived with her family and enjoyed doing so rather than living alone. That didn't fit the type of woman Justin would normally be attracted to.

"A workaholic like me, right?" he guessed as Delia continued to search for something to tell him.

Actually that wasn't far from the truth—close enough to agree. "It seems so."

"You'd better watch out. I was like you a couple of years ago and you know something?"

Delia shook her head, then remembered he couldn't see her. "What?"

"It's not worth it."

"But I like my job."

"It shouldn't be your life."

Then I wouldn't have much of a life at all, Delia thought miserably.

"Come on, are you going to admit that there's not one thing you do that isn't work-related?"

"I'm a tutor in the Tyler literacy program." So the meetings were held at the library. That wasn't cheating much.

"There you go. Now, what do you do for you?"

"For me?"

"Down time. How do you decompress?"

"I daydream," she admitted into the dark.

JUSTIN WAS UNEXPECTEDLY charmed. "About what? White knights sweeping you up on their chargers and taking you away from it all? Prince Charming rescuing you from wicked stepsisters?"

"Do I sound like someone who needs to be rescued?" she asked crossly.

"Maybe from a life of too much work and too little play."

"Everyone indulges in a rescue fantasy once in a while. I bet you do."

He could afford to rescue himself, but he didn't want to say that. "Maybe I do."

"Didn't you want to be rescued from those women earlier?"

"That wasn't a fantasy. That was a nightmare."

She didn't ask why they were chasing him, which he found curious. Unless she already knew. "Were you with those women?"

"No!"

"That was a very emphatic denial."

"Please. You weren't the only one being chased."

He blinked several times in the dark, as

though doing so would make her visible. "Why were they chasing you?"

"I'm in charge of a Valentine's Day charity event."

"I've heard that those charity dos can be very competitive." His mother was in charge of an animal shelter fund-raiser once and had said never again.

"That's one way to describe it."

"And another way?"

He heard her draw a breath. "As a way to support a good cause."

"I hear you. That's what got me into this mess in the first place. You know, when this is all over, I'm going on a vacation, far, far away."

"Where?"

He heard the eager curiosity in her voice, but he'd just been speaking rhetorically.

"I don't know. What would you pick?"

"Do I have to have actually been there?"

"Only if you intend to make hotel recommendations."

"I won't do that." She laughed. "Greece. I'd like to see Greece."

"Greece is nice."

"You've been there?" Her voice held a wistful enthusiasm.

"Yes."

"And all you can say is that it's nice? What about all the ruins? The art? The...the food?"

Many minutes later, Justin had told her everything he remembered about his trip to Greece. More than everything.

"What did it smell like?"

"Garlic and sweaty tourists."

"No! I mean, when you were in the ruins, could you sense the age? Did they *smell* old? Could you tell that people had once lived there?"

"You're a romantic, aren't you?"

"Yes, and I'm proud of it."

"Why?"

She had a ready answer. "Because people don't give the dreamers of the world enough credit. If we forget how to dream, then our civilization will stagnate. And we shouldn't forget that other people in other times had dreams, too. Sometimes I wonder if by visiting the places where they lived, I could dream their dreams, too."

Justin swallowed, aware that he'd never look at his travels in the same way ever again.

"Where else have you been?" she asked eagerly. "Paris? Have you been to Paris?"

He had and this time, when he described it, he tried to remember how it had smelled. She had him tell how the light shone through cathedral stained-glass windows, and was delighted when he mentioned the wear in the center of stone steps.

As he described other places he'd visited, he wished he could be there when she saw them for the first time.

"WHAT DO YOU MEAN you've never been ice-skating? Everybody's been ice-skating!"

"Not when you've grown up in Southern California. The lines are too long at the mall."

"Mall? You don't skate at a mall. You wait until the pond at your grandmother's freezes over."

"You'd wait a long time in Sun City, Arizona."

"BUT THEY BUTCHERED the book! The movie version cut three of the main characters and changed the setting from New York to Los Angeles."

"I read that book. The car chases only improved it. Could have used another explosion right at the end, though."

"You cannot be serious."

"I am. The book had no plot."

"Yes it did! It was about the lives of four struggling actors and what they'd do for their art."

"But only one of them did anything interesting."

"WAIT A MINUTE—YOU mean that you wear a foam rubber wedge of cheese on your head when you watch football?"

"As would any loyal Packer fan."

"But...cheese?"

"I think you have to be there."

"TELL ME HOW YOU became involved with the Special Olympics," she said.

Justin had lost all track of time and didn't care. He'd been talking to a voice in the dark. Darkness almost as complete as an underground cavern. A tiny sliver of light framed the doorway and extended a gray glow that didn't reach beyond the top step.

He had no idea of the outward appearance of his fellow refugee, but knew more about her in an hour or so than he'd learned about Beth in months of casual dating.

This woman had learned more about him—about what made him tick—than other women ever did, but probably didn't realize it. He found that the darkness and the sexy timbre of her voice were a therapeutic combination. She was a good listener and he took advantage until a nagging sense of fair play asserted itself.

But after sharing a tantalizing tidbit or two about herself, she always turned the conversation back to him.

She hadn't asked his name and he hadn't offered, relaxing under the cloak of anonymity. She wasn't blinded by all the trappings that went with being Justin Archer, and there'd been trappings even before the *American Woman* cover.

"A millionaire with style," he'd been called and enjoyed living up to the label. Why not? He'd worked hard, building his company from scratch like other computer firms. He still worked hard—or he did when he wasn't being hounded by the press and women who wanted to bear his children.

And, yes, he'd had plenty of offers. A shocking number of those were only interested in his "genetic contribution" as one letter put it.

It made him wonder how many other men in his situation had received offers like that and how many had accepted.

"You haven't answered my question."

"You've asked a lot of questions." And he'd answered them. There was something about her voice. It curled itself around him like smoke and made him willing to talk, willing to share parts of himself without wondering about her reaction. Maybe it was because he couldn't see her reaction.

"If you're tired of talking, then we don't have to."

But he wanted to talk. "I've done plenty of talking about me. It's your turn."

"I don't need a turn and I really want to hear about the Special Olympics."

He conceded for the moment. "I used to swim in college and one of my teammates became a weekend sports anchor in San Francisco. He recruited me."

"It's a wonderful thing to do."

He heard the admiration in her voice. Without facial expressions to go by, he found himself listening to inflection more than he ever had before. "Actually, the kids are the ones who're wonderful. The folks who care for them say you get back more than you give and they're right. I find it grounds me to take the time to work with them."

"It's still a wonderful thing to do, giving your time like that."

"Don't make me out to be some kind of saint." He didn't want her going all gushy on him.

She laughed. "I can't see you so I can make you out to be whomever I want!"

"What shall I make you out to be? Hmm?" He wondered what she looked like and wished that he didn't.

She didn't answer and he got the sense that she was upset by the question.

He answered for her. "You're a Wisconsin woman for starters. I can tell by the accent, not to mention your strange taste in hats."

She laughed. "Wisconsin born and bred."

"And therefore used to the winters. I'm picturing a sturdy, rosy-cheeked lass, broad-shouldered from shoveling all that snow. Is that right?''

She'd started giggling halfway through his nonsense. It made him feel good to hear her laugh.

''No! Except I am used to the winters, I guess.''

''No rosy cheeks?''

''Okay, maybe sometimes.''

''How about the broad shoulders?''

''I don't think so.''

''You don't know?''

She laughed again. ''What's your best stroke?''

She was trying to change the subject again, but he wasn't going to let her. ''You mean swimming stroke?''

''Is there another kind?''

He lowered his voice. ''There are many other kinds and I'm a master of them all.''

There was a short silence and then she spoke in strangled voice. ''Seriously, your swim stroke.''

Chicken Justin thought. ''Seriously, the butterfly, for which *my* broad shoulders come in handy. And that reminds me that we haven't established the breadth of *your* shoulders.''

Okay, it was a teenaged-boy-at-the-movies move, but he reached out into the darkness and draped his arm around her shoulders. Scratchy fabric met his fingers. "Hey, you're wearing a coat! No fair. I thought we were both silently freezing our...selves and you were being a real trooper.''

"Are you cold?" she asked.

"Yes, I'm cold! We're in a basement in Wisconsin in the dead of winter.''

"Do you want to share my coat?''

He slowly withdrew his arm. He wasn't *that* cold, but... "Yeah.''

Out of the darkness came the sounds of buttons moving through fabric. The sounds of a woman undressing. For him.

Get a grip.

The coat shrugged off her shoulders. Justin attempted to help her but ended up with a handful of sleeve.

"Thanks, but I'd better do this.''

She shifted against him and whatever grip he had slipped away as the warmth of her coat settled over half his back.

"How's that?"

That was pretty damn good. "Better."

He smelled wool and an underlying light, un-complicated perfume, one he didn't recognize, except that it was different from the heavy, complex perfume Beth wore. A perfume Justin had always thought was very sexy. He liked the way the scent changed as it faded, revealing different layers and inviting him closer to smell them.

Sitting there, surrounded by the faint echoes of another woman's perfume, Justin was struck by a truth: Beth's perfume was more complex than she was. On a subconscious level, he must have sensed this and that was what had been holding him back from proposing to her. He'd been aware that he didn't love her deeply, certainly not as deeply as he wanted to love the woman he planned to spend the rest of his life with. Now he knew, that for him at least, there wasn't enough to love.

All this from a whiff of a simple perfume worn by a woman of unexpected depth.

"Are you warm enough?"

It was too easy. "We'll need to sit closer to-gether," he said.

"Closer?"

Yes, he was aware of the fact that their hips and thighs were pressed against each other and the longer they'd talked, the more aware he'd become. "Just lean into me a little more—here." Reaching underneath the coat, he put his arm around her shoulders and turned slightly.

For one brief, crazy moment, when she leaned her head against his shoulder, Justin felt as though a piece missing from his life had dropped into place.

He drew an unsteady breath, and in the next instant, she'd straightened, holding herself with a telling stiffness.

This was a new situation. Women usually didn't object to being this close to Justin. Anyway, sharing the coat had been her idea, he told himself.

But you're the one who's trying to parlay it into something more. And not having any luck for the first time since his ill-fated attempt to date twins.

He was used to his good looks paving the way, and once he'd begun accumulating wealth, the way was not only paved, it was a six-lane superhighway.

But she didn't know she was supposed to find

him outwardly attractive, so he had to work on the inner attraction. He guessed this was supposed to be one of those overrated, character-building moments in his life.

Well, now there was an awkward silence between them. Should he apologize, or ignore the awkwardness in hopes that it would go away? He'd discovered—in another character-building moment—that apologies sometimes made a situation worse.

"I like books," she said out of nowhere.

How embarrassing.

Delia had felt guilty that Justin was cold because she was selfishly keeping them in the basement when she knew a few whacks above the doorknob would get them out.

She should have just given him the coat as penance, except that she knew he was too much of a gentleman to accept it. Then she'd heard herself offering to share, like it was a blanket and they were at a football game.

And he'd agreed.

Well, of course he'd agreed, because all he was after was warmth, whereas she...

Whereas she was after Justin Archer.

Pitiful, just pitiful.

She could barely unbutton her coat because she was shaking from the effort of not flinging herself against him and begging him to take her now. And the sad thing was that she was resisting the flinging, not because of any morals she might have once had, but because she was liable to send them both over the edge of the stairs onto the concrete floor of the basement.

She'd never wanted to touch another human being so much in her life—and be touched by him in turn, of course. Especially be touched by him in turn—lots of turns.

To distract herself, she kept playing conversational hopscotch, hoping to find something that would make Justin Archer a less attractive man.

A little while ago, she'd jumped into politics and discovered that he was a political conservative—except on the issues most important to her liberal views. And, she found herself reluctantly agreeing that he had valid points on issues where he disagreed with her. He didn't seem to have ego issues tied up with being right all the time.

Delia was becoming desperate. She had to

find *something* not to like about him. Sure, he was a little arrogant, but it came off as an attractive self-assurance. And he was a bit of a smooth talker, but was that enough to condemn him?

Not for her.

She was going to get hurt over this, but was way past the point of caring.

He was probably visualizing a nice, local woman, while she, who knew what he looked like, could fix an exact image in her head. And what image did she choose? Why, the poster of him in the itty-bitty swimsuit, naturally.

There was a finite amount of time a woman could visualize that poster and not want to take advantage of the fact that she was alone with the man who'd posed for it. Delia's time was up.

And so, when she'd found herself maneuvered next to the chest she'd daydreamed over, she'd nestled against it. *Nestled,* her eyes closed, a smile on her lips, a song in her heart, et cetera, et cetera.

He was warm, in spite of his protests, and his heart beat with steady thuds that made her feel safe and cherished.

Then he'd gone still, making her aware of what she'd done.

She'd ruined everything—ruined the teasing and the confiding and the easy way they'd been talking with each other.

Delia was almost in tears, which was stupid. Besides, crying women annoyed him. "I like books," she burst out, then held her breath, wishing she'd eased into her ace-in-the-hole topic with more finesse.

"So do I." She heard him smile. "So do I."

CHAPTER SIX

JUSTIN'S ARM WAS starting to go to sleep, but he didn't want to move it from around her shoulders for fear that she'd pull away. It had taken far too long to get her to relax against him, not that he hadn't enjoyed the process.

The more they talked, especially during their book discussions, and the more he learned about her, the more he wanted to know.

He wanted to know what his mystery woman of the dark looked like. He wished that it didn't matter to him, but it did, and not because he needed to know to be attracted to her. That was the thing. He was already attracted to her; that's why he wanted to know what she looked like.

By some sneaky questioning, he'd pinned her age as near to his own. He also knew that in spite of her ultra sexy voice, she wasn't sophisticated in a worldly way, or the same worldly way he was. That wasn't to say she was naive or burdened with an exclusionary small-town mentality, either.

He'd never met anyone like her and he wanted more. Okay, he'd admit it—he wanted to kiss her for starters. There was nothing wrong with that, but without being able to see each other, there was no way for her to guess his intentions and let him know whether she was willing or not.

He supposed he could just come out and ask but surely he could come up with a better approach.

"You know," she said, "I'm beginning to think we've missed lunch."

"I thought that a while ago. How are you doing? Warm enough?" He gave her shoulder a brisk rub to disguise the fact that he was flexing his arm to regain some feeling.

Maybe he was too brisk. She moved her head and his chin crashed into something soft. He guessed it was her nose. Reflexively, he reached out and connected with her hair. "Are you okay?"

She sniffed. "Ouch," she said in a tiny voice.

"I'm sorry. That was your nose, wasn't it?"

"It's okay."

His hand was on her cheek. Rather than taking it away, he rubbed his thumb across her skin. "You sure? It might be bleeding."

"You didn't hit it that hard."

"I'm glad." His thumb swept across her cheek again, gently outlining the shape of the bone. "You have soft skin," he whispered.

"Thank you."

Slowly, Justin brought his other hand across her back and up the side of her neck until his fingers touched her other cheek.

"What are you doing?" she whispered and he felt the warmth of her breath puff against his neck.

He tilted her face up ever so slightly. "I'm seeing what you look like."

Her fingers wrapped themselves around his wrists.

"Please?" he asked.

"Only if I get a turn, too."

He smiled with satisfaction. "Absolutely."

Slowly, her hands fell away and he felt her draw a shaky breath. "Are you nervous?" he asked.

"A little."

"It's not like I'm a braille expert, or anything."

"No, but you're a woman expert."

His hands slid to her shoulders. "How did you know?"

"We've been talking for hours—how couldn't I know?"

And she was afraid she wouldn't measure up, he surmised. "I'm not thinking about other women right now. I'm thinking of you."

She moved his hands back to her face. Hers were cold.

"You have high cheekbones."

"And a tender nose," she reminded him as his fingers wandered in that direction.

He gently traced the bridge of it several times, noting that it was straight without the slight hump in the middle that his had.

He discovered full eyebrows and a prominent brow bone. He longed to ask her the color of her eyes, but decided that would be cheating. Her hair was thick and wavy and ended somewhere between her ear and her shoulder. Justin traced the shape of her ears, lingering at the lobes. She had pierced ears and wore tiny ball earrings.

He'd deliberately saved her mouth for last. "You're lovely," he murmured as he drew his fingers down her jawline.

"But—"

"Shh." He held a finger against her mouth, then, with the gentlest of touches, traced the outline of her lips.

Her breath came quickly, telling him she wasn't unaffected by his explorations.

Justin lingered at her lips until they parted. He leaned forward, ready to substitute his mouth for his finger, when she spoke.

"My turn."

DELIA'S LIPS BURNED and tingled and she couldn't stand any more of Justin's touch.

Her eyes had started to tear with frustration and she knew if the tears spilled over, he'd feel them on her cheeks.

Blinking in the dark, Delia started with her hands in the same position as Justin's.

"You have a thick beard!"

"It's a pain. More often than not, I have to shave twice a day."

The roughness served to sensitize her fingers. She drew them over his jaw and purposely sought out the crescent scar on his chin. "What happened here?"

"I hit the diving board trying to do a backwards flip."

"Ouch."

She felt his smile. "Didn't stop me from slapping a bandage on it and practicing all afternoon. I probably should have had stitch or two."

"I think it makes you look interesting."

"Look?" he asked.

Delia realized her slip. "I have a picture in my mind," she told him. Which she did. It just happened to be poster-sized.

She thought of that poster, as well as his cover photo on *American Woman* as she traced the contours of his face. She moved slowly, drawing out the contact as much as possible.

Her empty stomach told her that Molly must have eaten lunch out, which meant she'd be back to start preparing tea shortly. Delia's time with Justin was quickly drawing to a close.

She desperately wished she had enough courage to just kiss him. He'd probably kiss her back, too.

"Have you got a thing for ears?"

"Sorry. I was thinking." She moved her

hands from his ears down his jawline toward his mouth. "They did feel like cute ears, though."

He laughed.

And then he placed the tiniest, softest kiss against her fingers. It was barely a movement of his mouth at all, which meant it was probably wishful thinking on her part.

Her fingers stilled and one hand fell away. She wished, *wished* she could look into his eyes. With her heart pounding in her ears, she traced his upper lip.

Justin inhaled sharply, then deliberately pressed her fingers against his mouth and kissed them, and this time there was no mistaking it as a kiss.

Then he pressed them against her own mouth.

Delia just stopped herself from saying his name.

An instant later, his lips met hers.

This was so very different from kissing a poster, was her first and only thought for long while.

Without breaking the kiss, Justin drew her into his arms, and in that instant, he entered her, heart and soul, though he'd never know it.

It was a magical moment and Delia tried to

notice everything about it so she would always remember. His beard was rough against her cheek, but not overly so—just enough to sensitize the nerve endings.

She loved the way one hand held her against him while the other cradled the back of her head.

And she especially loved the feel of his mouth against hers.

Once, at a relative's wedding, Delia, who didn't consider herself much of a dancer, danced with an older uncle of the groom, a man who made ballroom dancing his hobby. He'd been kind to pay attention to the teenaged Delia, and she'd quickly learned that when dancing with a master, she was better than she'd ever been before.

Kissing was a lot like dancing.

And Justin was a master. As she had with the ballroom dancer all those years ago, Delia simply relaxed and let him take the lead.

"I've been wanting to do that for hours," he murmured, still holding her close.

"Is it over already?"

"No way."

This time, he urged her lips apart, seeking, and getting, a response from her. Delia eagerly met his tongue with hers, reveling in the sensation.

A low guttural noise rumbled in his chest as she pressed against him.

"This...is incredible," he breathed.

"No talking. Only kissing."

But as Delia soon discovered, only kissing, though wonderful, was very limiting.

Justin buried his mouth at the side of her neck and murmured things that gave her shivers. His hands moved over her, slowly, so slowly, that when he finally did touch her breasts, Delia thought she would explode.

She couldn't breathe anymore and her lungs ached. All of her ached.

"So sweet," Justin murmured and began unbuttoning her jumper.

Delia felt recklessly crazed with wanting. Nothing mattered to her except Justin's touch.

Nothing except the sound of voices.

It was her imagination. It had to be.

Justin stilled, his breathing heavy. "Did you hear something?"

Delia murmured a protest and drew his mouth back to hers. She became bolder, unbuttoning his shirt and running her hands over his chest.

She pressed kisses near his throat, burying her nose against him and inhaling his scent. She wanted to remember everything about him— wanted these last precious seconds.

"Hey, sweetheart, I did hear something. Listen."

She didn't have to listen hard. Delia squeezed back tears. "Yeah," she managed and began fastening the buttons on her jumper.

From the sounds she heard, Justin was redoing his own buttons.

"So we get to see each other at last."

"Yeah." Delia's heart felt like a lump of lead in her chest.

"I...I need to tell you something."

"Please don't."

The voices drew closer. Delia identified Molly and Sara. Moments later, they were joined by Quinn. Any second now, and one of them would discover the closed basement door.

Delia had thought about what she would do when this moment arrived so that she could leave without Justin seeing her. After all they'd shared, she couldn't bear to see the disappointment on his face.

Oh, he'd be too polite to show it, but he

wouldn't be able to fake a sparkle in his eye, or the special quality she'd heard in his voice.

He'd know immediately that in spite of their inner compatibility, the reality was that they were a mismatch. He wouldn't want to hurt her and pretending that it didn't matter would inflict the biggest hurt of all.

And that was assuming he could get past the fact that she'd known who he was all along and hadn't told him, which he was bound to discover sooner or later. Probably sooner.

No, better to stick to her plan. At least that way, she'd get to keep her fantasy.

"Sounds like the cavalry has arrived." He didn't seem all that excited, but that could be wishful thinking on her part.

"And it's a good thing, too." She tried to sound bright and nonchalant. "I think I'm numb from sitting so long." Which was a lie. She was anything but numb.

"Look…"

He was gearing up for an "It's been swell, but so long" speech.

She didn't want to hear it. "Can't look—it's dark!"

He gave an unwilling laugh. "What I'm trying to say—hey, I don't even know your name."

And she wanted to keep it that way. Little Sara's chattering sounded clearly now. They must be right outside. Delia wiggled her shoe loose and nudged it over the edge. "Oh, no—my shoe!"

"I'll get it for you," he offered, just as she'd planned. "Hold the door so the light will shine down."

"Sure," Delia agreed.

At the same instant, she heard Molly exclaim, "Who shut this door?"

It was all going exactly as she'd hoped it would, wasn't it? Delia quickly climbed up the stairs. "Molly!" She felt for the knob and pounded the door just above it. "Molly, we're in here!"

Delia pounded again to cover up Molly's surprised, "Delia!"

Whether Delia's pounding had the desired effect, or whether Molly's thwack on her side did the trick didn't matter. The door flew open.

And Delia slammed it shut again against a quickly muffled, "Hey!"

"Delia, what—"

Delia grabbed both her arms. "I don't have time to explain. Don't tell Justin who I am. Swear you won't, Molly."

"De—"

"Swear!"

"All right, all right."

"Give me a head start, then let him out, okay?"

"Sure, but—"

"I'll explain it all someday."

"You'll explain it all when I call you this evening!"

"Miss Delia—you lost your shoe."

"I know, Sara. I'll get it later."

Delia waved and limped past a startled Quinn toward the foyer, her shoeless foot already cold.

HE THOUGHT THEY HAD the beginning of something special. In fact, they were well into the middle of something special and Justin very much wanted to continue that something special and soon.

"Just tell me where I can find her," he demanded of Molly.

"She didn't want you to know."

That made absolutely no sense. "Did she say

that, or did she just ask you not to tell me her name?''

Molly looked miserable. ''I know she meant that she didn't want to see you.''

''But if she didn't *say*—''

''Mr. Archer, please! I'm in a very awkward position. Only you two know what went on between you in that basement, so only you can figure out the reason that she doesn't want to be known.''

''We talked,'' Justin told her quietly. ''And we connected on a level I've never felt with any other woman. And I'm not walking away from that.''

Molly's eyes teared. ''Oh, that's so beautiful. What is wrong with that girl?''

''Just tell me where I can find her. A hint.''

Molly shook her head. ''But I'll talk to her for you.''

And Justin knew that was the only concession he was going to get. ''Make it soon.''

''DON'T YOU DARE TELL him, Molly!'' It was Sunday and Molly had called four times already.

''Delia, you're being an idiot. Justin Archer is desperate to find you and you're hiding! I don't get it!''

Once more, Delia tried to explain. "He thinks I'm somebody I'm not. Somebody witty and sophisticated and...and pretty."

"You are pretty," Molly insisted, correctly identifying Delia's key concern.

"You have to say that. You're my friend. Anyway, I'm talking about his kind of pretty— the gorgeous kind that makes men drool in the streets. That's what he's used to. When he sees me...well, he's not going to see me."

"Then talk to him on the phone."

"No."

"He'll leave today and you won't ever see him again."

Delia closed her eyes as tightly as possible, trying to recreate the dark. "Yes, I will."

"Delia—he doesn't believe I've talked to you!"

"Tell him...tell him 'plastics.'"

HE SHOULD HAVE TOLD her who he was. He should have made her listen. No woman in her right mind would reject Justin Archer.

But that was cynical of him, and unworthy of her. Besides, that was Justin Archer lite. He'd shown her the real Justin Archer.

And she wouldn't even talk to him.

It wasn't just his pride that was hurt. His emotions had taken a hit that was going to take him some time to get over. Any man who kept a woman's shoe…

What had he done wrong? Molly had told him she wasn't married, so that wasn't the problem. And why wouldn't she just talk to him?

He could find her if he tried hard enough, but why should he try when she clearly didn't want anything more to do with him?

There was nothing for him to do but to go back to San Francisco.

Once he'd decided to leave, Justin packed quickly. He'd rather spend the night in the airport hotel in Madison than stay here.

He was zipping up his carry-on when there was a knock on the door. It was Molly and she held an envelope.

"I found this in your mailbox downstairs. The other guests also received one."

He took the envelope and saw that it was addressed to Richard Longfield. Probably some advertisement. He tossed the envelope on the nightstand.

"Open it," Molly urged from the doorway. She was smiling.

Justin ripped it open. "This is an invitation to some carnival at the library."

"You ought to go."

"Sorry." He shook his head and tossed the invitation into the trash. "As you can see, I'm going to check out now."

"You really ought to go," she repeated. Coming into the room, she retrieved the paper and tapped the signature at the bottom. "You've received a personal invitation."

There was something about her voice and the significant look she gave him. Justin studied the signature. Delia Mayhew. "Have I met Ms. Mayhew?" he asked softly.

Molly beamed. "Yes, I believe you have."

VALENTINE'S DAY AND her heart was broken. So what else was new?

Well, Delia was staring out at a library parking lot that was so full, people had to park on the side streets. That was new.

In addition, the library staff had filled out a record number of library card applications and Delia had made her sixth urn of coffee. She'd borrowed a lectern and raised platform from the high school and she'd decorated with so much crepe paper, she thought her fingers were going to be permanently stained red.

The chairs in the reading area were full and had been for some time with the ladies of Tyler's upper crust staking out the best spots. They'd proved to be as aggressive as any other female in Tyler. Delia could hardly blame them. Justin was... She sighed. Justin was a wonderful memory. Painful, heart wrenching, and setting an impossibly high standard for any other man, but wonderful.

And she'd do it all over again in a heartbeat. Probably more.

She knew the big turnout was due to the persistent rumor that he was going to make an appearance. Nothing she said would stop it.

She'd found no one else. No one. She'd called for hours. Eventually, she raided her savings, drove to an exclusive Madison toy store and bought a six-foot stuffed Cheeboo.

That was going to be the special guest.

Other than Bobo. He'd been so sweet and she felt so awful. After Saturday, she just knew those women wouldn't be shy about expressing their disappointment.

Delia had tried to make it up to Bobo in advance and he'd unfortunately misinterpreted her actions and had asked her out for dinner.

And so, last night, she'd endured an excruciating dinner in which she and Bobo Boleski learned that they had nothing in common. As Bobo said when he told her good night, "No harm, no foul."

"Hey Delia, when are you going to get this show on the road?" a woman from the front row asked.

The women had been lined up waiting to get into the library when it opened at ten o'clock, even though Delia hadn't planned to start the main activities until two o'clock, with the speakers beginning at four.

They'd drunk lots of coffee—free today only—and had eaten most of the cheese samples.

"We've already started. There's face painting and you can make a Valentine for your honey in the children's section. In young adults, there's going to be a raffle for three autographed copies of *The Monster Car from Brisbane* and free bookmarks. We have a wreath-making demonstration by Mary McNally, author of *Wreaths for all Occasions* and, courtesy of the Wisconsin Cheese Indus—"

"Bring him on, honey. We're tired of waiting."

Delia swallowed. "Ten minutes."

The jazz band from the high school launched into "Sing Sing Sing" and drowned out the grumbling.

The library was packed with people, just the way she'd hoped.

And in ten minutes, they'd all turn against her.

Delia escaped into her office and stared at the poster of Justin Archer for luck. She still couldn't believe she'd met him, let alone kissed him and run her fingers over that incredible chest.

But she'd made the right decision. She had only good memories now, whereas if he'd seen her... She'd just enjoy the good memories.

Delia rose and knocked on Elise's office door, where Bobo was waiting, patiently playing computer solitaire. "We'll have three guests before you. Listen for your intro."

Bobo nodded. He knew the drill. "I read a book. Should I say something about it?"

"Sure." Why not?

Delia smoothed her hair, plastered on a smile, and made her way to the podium.

"Ladies and gentlemen." Or mostly ladies. "Welcome to the Alberta Ingalls Memorial Library's Book Lovers' Day. We're pleased to have with us Gloria Dowd, head librarian at the University of Wisconsin…"

There was barely polite applause until Elise strode to the front of the room and gave the women her best librarian's glare.

Applause for Ms. Dowd increased.

Mercifully, she kept her remarks short, as did the high school principal and the mayor's wife.

"And now, we have a very special guest," Delia began. "Someone we don't normally think of when we think of libraries and books."

The crowd began to murmur excitedly. Delia saw that many of them were getting copies of *American Woman* ready.

"Someone who has supported Tyler programs before," Delia said, to warn them. "Someone we're always glad to see," she continued and the murmuring died down a little. "Let's give a big Tyler welcome to Bobo Boleski!" Delia applauded wildly and the jazz band started playing the school fight song.

Bobo jogged out of her office, high-fiving people all the way.

There was a stunned silence from the front row.

"Hey, kids!" he shouted.

"Hey, Bobo!" they shouted back from the far side where they'd been stashed by their mothers.

"You know, I read a book once."

Delia swallowed hard, her smile still pinned to her face.

"It's called *The Art of War* and it was written a bunch of years ago by some Chinese dude. Now, my coach had to make me read this book, 'cause I gotta tell ya, I wasn't interested in what any old Chinaman had to say. But you know something? He was a smart old guy. And his book was about war, but it was about more than war, you know? It was strategies, strategies that we used to make up plays when I played hockey for the Razors."

A cheer went up, led by the band's drummer.

"I found myself remembering what that old guy had to say even after I played hockey. And I read that book again. In fact, I've probably read it four times. And you know, it makes me think. That's what books do. They make you think. And when you think, you're just better at whatever you do.''

Delia felt tears again, and when Bobo finished a few minutes later to more applause than when he'd entered, Delia walked up to him and gave him a big kiss on the cheek right in front of everybody.

"And we have one more special guest," she said, and signaled Pauline and Elise to carry in the stuffed Cheeboo.

Shrieks of delight from the children almost drowned out the noise in the foyer as a knight in armor, wearing a helmet with a white plume, pushed open the glass doors.

As Delia stared, he came clanking right toward her, carrying a red velvet pillow topped by a white, cloth-covered lump. Slipping in behind him was Molly.

She glanced over at Elise and Pauline, but they seemed as mystified as she was.

The room was silent, except for the happy noise from the youngest children who were madly hugging Cheeboo.

The knight approached and presented the velvet pillow to Delia. With a flourish, he removed the cloth to reveal…

"A shoe?" asked one of the women.

Delia clamped her hands over her mouth. That wasn't just any shoe. That was her dress flat, which meant… Her knees started shaking, probably from lack of oxygen, since she wasn't breathing, either.

The knight set the pillow on the podium and used both hands to remove his helmet.

Justin Archer, hair unkempt, grinned down at her. "Greetings fair maid of the dark."

"Justin," she whispered. "What—how—"

He held his finger to his lips. "After my speech." He gazed at her a moment longer, then turned and bowed to the crowd, which erupted into screams.

From the frenzy, he might have been a rock star. As it was, the sheriff and two deputies had to calm everyone down. Delia didn't know who'd alerted them, but was glad they had.

"All my life I've loved books and lately, I've begun collecting old volumes—not because I want them, but because I want to protect them— to restore and preserve them." He continued, talking about how important books were to him and to the future. During his remarks, he casually signed copies of his *American Woman* cover.

Delia had no idea what he said. She was having enough trouble grasping the fact that he was here at all and that he knew who she was. She tried to catch Molly's eye, but Molly wouldn't look at her.

"And now, you're probably wondering why I'm in this getup." He flashed a smile guaranteed to melt steel—or armor. "This *is* Valentine's Day and I *am* a lover—"

Hoots and whistles interrupted him. He shook his finger playfully. "A *book* lover—what were you thinking?"

"I'm thinking you should come home with me!" a woman called out.

Justin laughed. "Lately, I've also discovered that I'm a believer in dreams and fairy tales." He turned to Delia. "And happily ever afters with true soul mates."

With that, he bent down and picked her up. Gasps and laughter sounded from the crowd.

"Justin!"

He started carrying her through the crowd. "Yes, *Delia?*"

"You know my name."

"And you know my name."

She hesitated, then confessed. "I always knew your name."

"Yeah, I figured as much. You're forgiven, so quit looking at me as though I'm going to drop you."

"Well..."

Grinning, Justin shifted her and Delia wrapped her arms around his neck to take some of the weight off her back and legs.

Armor was romantic, but not very comfortable.

"I can't believe you're here," she murmured, not sure whether he could hear her above the creaking of the armor.

"You invited me."

She'd forgotten. "But—"

"Fantasies work best when you don't question the details too closely."

Good point.

Someone opened the door for them and Justin carried her outside to the parking lot where a carriage pulled by two white horses waited.

Delia could only stare. Behind her, she heard the exclamations and applause from the crowd who'd followed them. Justin set her on the lowered steps and she climbed onto the red leather seat. He climbed in after her and wrapped her in soft blankets.

"Armor's cold, in case you wondered," he said and she gave him one of her blankets.

"I can't believe you did all this."

"You weren't responding to the more conventional methods and then I realized that it was because you weren't a conventional woman."

"It was because I'm not the type of woman a man like you would want."

"You are exactly the type of woman I want."

Delia looked into his eyes and the way they gazed steadily into hers. She heard the sincerity in his voice, but she still couldn't quite believe him.

Then he leaned down and kissed her.

And she believed him.

But then, he was a very good kisser.

The driver raised the steps and took his place. As he clicked the reins and the horses began clopping on the asphalt, Delia and Justin waved goodbye to the crowd at the library.

"Where are we going?" she asked.

Justin grinned. "To the land of happily ever after."

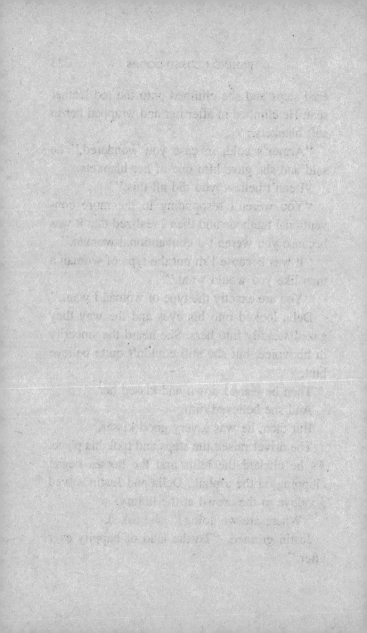

THE BRIDE'S SURPRISE

Jacqueline Diamond

CHAPTER ONE

IT WAS GOING TO BE the perfect wedding, Rebecca Salber told herself as she smoothed the white satin skirt of her bridal gown and stepped from the hotel elevator.

She'd known since she was a little girl that she wanted a big wedding with loads of flowers, devoted bridesmaids and a man who would never let her down. A sweet, kind man with whom to share her life.

In another two hours, her dream would come true. Then she and her new husband would head for a cozy honeymoon of unimaginable bliss. Having saved herself for twenty-seven years, Rebecca was more than ready to experience the joyous revelations that lovemaking would bring.

The day after tomorrow was Valentine's Day, and she would be enjoying it as a newlywed. If only the holiday had fallen on a Saturday instead of a Monday, she might even have been a Valentine's Day bride. On the other hand, who wanted a red wedding dress?

Rebecca frowned at this unromantic image. She didn't intend to let anything mar her perfect day, not even a wayward thought.

Hurrying through the dark-beamed, English-style lobby, she headed for the banquet manager's office. There'd been some mix-up about the band hired to play at the reception, but Rebecca was certain it could be straightened out.

After all, Swan's Folly was the poshest hotel in Lake Geneva, Wisconsin, and Rebecca's mother was the assistant manager. Having grown up nearby, Rebecca knew the staff's reputation for perfection. In fact, that was one of the reasons she'd chosen to stage her wedding here instead of in Madison, where she lived.

She broke stride at the sight of the tuxedo-clad man staring at her from across the lobby. Tall, with black hair and riveting blue eyes, he held himself with a touch of arrogance.

The commanding presence of Rick Travis was enough to take any woman's breath away. And the way he was studying Rebecca made her feel every inch a woman, from her tingling lips to her suddenly taut breasts.

She smiled. "Hey, Rick, how's it going?" After all these years of friendship, she knew better than to take the guy seriously. He might bowl over every other woman who crossed his path, but not her.

He grinned back. "I'm not sure this 'man of honor' business sits well with your mother. She's been pointedly ignoring me."

Rebecca had to admit her mother hadn't taken well to the idea of inviting her best friend, who happened to be Rick, to replace the customary maid of honor. "She's crazy about Steve. She thinks it's insulting to have another guy standing next to me."

"I would never insult Steve. Even if he is only half my size." Rick winked lazily and stretched the broad shoulders that testified to his status as a former football star. His easygoing insults, which were reserved for Rebecca's ears alone, never failed to arouse a peppery response.

"Some women just don't fall for the Incredible Hulk," she said. "Galling, isn't it?"

"Water off a duck's back," he retorted.

"I'd love to stay here all day and throw darts at your ego, but I've got a little problem to take care of," Rebecca said. "See you later."

"Not if I see you first," he teased.

A woman walking out of the hotel restaurant took one look at him and stumbled right into her husband. Rick often had that effect on females, Rebecca reflected in amusement.

She'd reacted that way herself, the first time she saw him. Her sophomore year in college, she had accepted a girlfriend's suggestion that they share an apartment with Rick and his roommate. Having met only the other male roommate, she awoke the first morning and nearly suffered heart failure when she slogged into the kitchen and saw Mr. Dreamboat fixing breakfast.

Clad only in shorts, he'd been too hunky and masculine to ignore. Rebecca had stood there staring until her sense of self-preservation kicked in.

She'd snapped that he ought to have the decency to cover up. He'd grinned and said no one else had ever complained. That had been the start of a barbed but rewarding friendship.

Remembering her mission, Rebecca located Connie Graf, the banquet manager, in her office. A tall ash-blonde with Grace Kelly looks, Connie wore a relieved expression as she hung up the phone.

"It was just Joe's stupid idea of a joke. The band wasn't double-booked, and they'll be here on time," she said. "I hate that man! How can he imagine I'd ever reconcile with him? Believe me, Rebecca, you're wise to marry a considerate guy like Steve instead of a macho meathead."

Connie's estranged husband, Joe Graf, managed several bands in Lake Geneva. According to Rebecca's mother, she'd left him a month earlier, and he'd been alternately harassing her and begging for forgiveness ever since.

"I know," Rebecca said. "Steve will never let me down. That's why I picked him."

"He's such a charmer!" In the mirror of her compact, Connie checked her makeup. It was, as usual, flawless. "He's taken an interest in every detail of the seating arrangement and the luncheon menu. Most men couldn't care less about their wedding, let alone the reception."

"That's what makes him good at business." Steve was a computer consultant to the accounting firm where Rebecca worked, which was how they'd met. "He's starting his own Internet company, troubleshooting computers. Just e-mail or call him and he'll talk you through any problem you're having."

"He's going to make a million." Connie smiled enviously. "He's sweet *and* he's going to be rich. What a catch!"

Rebecca didn't care whether her husband made a million dollars, as long as he was reliable and loving. Having been abandoned by her father when she was six, she wanted better for her own children.

In fact, she wanted the best. And she was going to have him.

RICK ADJUSTED HIS bow tie, then wondered how to fill the next two hours. Any other maid of honor, he supposed, would be upstairs giggling with the bridesmaids, but he had no interest in doing that.

It occurred to him that, since Rebecca lacked a father to protect her, maybe he ought to seek out a man-to-man talk with Steve, of the "you do her wrong and I'll punch your lights out" variety. He doubted either the bride or the groom would appreciate his good intentions, however.

Instead, he wandered down the hall toward the ballroom. The hotel, he'd heard, had once been a private estate and was modeled after an English country house. Its cheery intimacy gave him the uneasy sense that he was intruding into someone else's home.

Or perhaps his uneasiness stemmed from a different source. At the entrance to Ballroom One, Rick paused to explore this train of thought.

He and Becky had been friends since they and two friends shared an apartment while attending the University of Wisconsin. Later, when he returned to Madison after playing professional football, they'd taken to eating lunch together several times a week, and sometimes hung out together in the evenings. Even so, they'd always known they were incompatible in any romantic sense.

Becky was too bossy and too sharp-tongued. As for her taste in entertainment, sure, he enjoyed the change of pace when he escorted her to the theater or a concert, and she cheered loud and long when he dragged her to football games, but who wanted a steady diet of someone else's preferences?

If they had been so foolish as to marry, they would have fought over everything from what to name the baby to what color to paint the front porch. Life would be downright brutal married to Becky, which was why Rick didn't envy Steve Whittman one iota.

Unfortunately, he didn't like the fellow very much, either. He'd always hoped that whomever Becky married could become Rick's good friend, too. That way, they could all go places together.

Still, he had no reason to dislike Steve, other than the fact that the man had once made a belittling remark about advertising executives before he learned that Rick was one. Other than that, Steve seemed intelligent, and most people found him pleasant company.

The guy was a little too smooth for Rick's taste, and he let Becky push him around, submitting without an argument while she made all the decisions. Becky needed a strong man, not a weak one.

But this was the husband she'd picked. If Rick intended to maintain their friendship, and he did, he would have to tolerate the fellow.

A movement across the room caught his attention. Diane Salber, Becky's mother, had entered through another door and was prowling the rows of white-draped chairs set up in front of the altar. Her peach-colored suit blended with the sprays of flowers in white, peach and maroon.

Before she could spot him, Rick slipped back into the hall and went to inspect Ballroom Two, which was half of the same oversized room separated by a divider. Here, round tables flanked a dance floor, with the bridal colors repeated in the linens and decorations. On a side table stood a multitiered cake topped by bride-and-groom dolls.

A tray of petits fours sat beside it. There weren't any bowls of nuts, since Rebecca was allergic to peanuts.

His stomach grumbling with midafternoon emptiness, Rick strode over and helped himself to a small green petit four from the back of the tray.

He was in the act of stuffing it into his mouth when Diane Salber entered. The woman was short, like Becky, with the same intense features in an entirely different palette. Where her daughter's vivid red locks and jade-green eyes brightened any scene, Diane's brunette coloring gave her a sterner cast.

Beneath the heat of her glare, he nearly choked. Rick hadn't felt like such a clumsy kid since his school days. In fact, Becky's mother reminded him a little of Pam Kelsey, his high school football coach in Tyler, Wisconsin. She used to regard him with that same exasperated expression during her first year as coach, when he'd given her a lot of trouble.

"I'm sorry, Mrs. Salber," he said after the petit four finished its trip down his throat. "I was hungry."

Now he had green goop on his fingers, Rick realized, and wondered how she would react if he used one of the monogrammed paper napkins. On the other hand, licking his fingers wasn't exactly suave.

"You know how I feel about Rebecca's decision to put you in the wedding." Diane brushed back a wing of brown hair that had escaped its French twist. "I won't belabor the point."

"I guess I must stick out like a sore thumb among the bridesmaids, huh?" Reaching behind his back, Rick scraped his smeared fingers across one of the napkins, then wondered how to dispose of the thing. "I promise, I'll do my best to fade into the background."

"It's nothing personal. Just remember which

man is center stage today." He knew that steely expression. It was the same one her daughter wore when she was determined to get her way. "I want Rebecca to have everything I missed out on. A man to take care of her, a lifetime of beautiful memories, and let's not forget financial security."

"And Steve's the guy," he prompted, determined to agree with her, no matter what she said. That was the way to pacify Becky, he'd learned, and it ought to work on her mother, too.

"That's right." She gave him a trace of a smile. "I've never been so impressed by a man. Steve is everything a mother could ask for."

"I'm not standing in the way." Crumpling the napkin behind him, Rick tried to figure out how to stuff it into his pocket. Then he remembered that the tuxedo didn't have a pocket.

"You'll make the wedding photos look odd, though." Diane tapped her fingers against the back of a chair. "That reminds me, where *is* the photographer? He should be here by now."

As she turned away, Becky stuck her head in the door. With her hair piled up, she looked more elegant than usual, and yet more vulnerable, too. "Has anybody seen my clipboard? I can't believe I lost it."

"You don't need a clipboard," her mother said. "I'll take care of the details from here on."

"But I feel naked without it," Becky protested. "I'll bet I left it in the bridal suite. I'll go check."

"Just stay away from Steve's wing!" Diane ordered. "It's bad luck for him to see you before the wedding."

"Nobody believes that anymore," Becky said. "See you later." She vanished into the hall, and her mother left a moment later.

Rick made one more survey of the empty room. In a few hours, it would fill with noisy guests, while the bride and groom beamed at the head table.

Then he would return, alone, to the house he'd bought in his hometown of Tyler. And, day after tomorrow, he would make the usual commute to Madison, but this time Becky wouldn't be meeting him for lunch, because she'd still be on her honeymoon.

It was enough to turn a man's stomach. Or make it growl.

With only a moment's hesitation, Rick

plucked another petit four from the tray and popped it into his mouth.

REBECCA DARTED UP the steps to the second floor. She tried to ignore the jolt she'd felt when she saw Rick standing beside the wedding cake and imagined for one blinding instant that he was the groom.

Her heart had lifted in a way she couldn't explain. She sure was going to miss him. Obviously, they couldn't spend as much time together once she was married. But it would be worth it, she reminded herself firmly.

Now, the clipboard. She hadn't taken it downstairs to Connie Graf's office, so it had to be upstairs.

But there was no sign of it in the bridal suite, Rebecca discovered when she arrived there. She racked her brain to remember where she'd seen the clipboard last.

Oh, yes, she'd taken it about an hour ago when she went to make sure the bridesmaids had received their bouquets. She'd stopped in first to see Ellen Pfeiffer, a fellow accountant, and then Cindy Olofson, a health club chum, both of whom lived in Madison.

Last, she'd made a point of spending a few minutes with Esther Breeland, her best friend from high school, a manicurist who still lived here in Lake Geneva. As the child of eastern European immigrants, Esther had felt like an outsider during her school days, and so had the fatherless Rebecca. Their friendship had meant a lot to them both.

She'd definitely checked off the bouquet in Esther's room. The clipboard was probably sitting on the bridesmaid's end table right now.

Rebecca locked her door and walked slowly down the hall. The closer the time came for her wedding, the more nervous she felt.

Hastily, her mind ran over the details of the coming ceremony and lunch reception, but there was nothing to worry about. Surely, if anything *had* been overlooked, Mom would take care of it.

And Rebecca had noticed earlier that, outside, a limousine was already waiting to whisk her and Steve to their honeymoon retreat. They'd chosen a bed and breakfast that Rick had recommended in his nearby hometown of Tyler.

Steve had dropped a few hints about going someplace more exciting, like Florida or Southern California, but Rebecca didn't want glamour. She needed to feel safe and secure when she took the plunge into the intimacies of married life. Besides, she was curious to see the friendly town she'd heard so much about.

At Esther's room, Rebecca rapped lightly. She heard a fluttery noise inside, but no one responded, so she knocked again. There was dead silence.

She stood debating what to do. Then the rustling resumed.

Once, in high school, Esther had fainted when she was coming down with the flu. Come to think of it, at breakfast this morning she had looked a bit flushed. Suppose she were lying on the floor right this minute, struggling to get up?

"Esther?" Rebecca tried the knob, and, to her surprise, the door opened. She stepped inside.

The covers dangled half-off the bed, revealing two people in an obvious state of disarray. In the instant before she averted her gaze, even an innocent like Rebecca could see clearly what they were up to. "I'm so sorry!"

Esther groped for the covers. "What are you doing here?"

The man kept his face averted, but his short,

light-brown hair looked familiar. He must be one of Steve's ushers, Becky thought as she swung toward the door.

There was a white tuxedo draped over a chair, she noticed in confusion. The groomsmen were wearing black. The only one dressed in a white tux would be...

"Steve?" The name seemed to stick in her larynx, but he must have heard her, because he turned.

Her heart rate speeded and her palms grew damp. This couldn't really be happening. The man she'd intended to marry in less than two hours couldn't be lying there naked in bed with another woman.

Despite her flaming cheeks, Rebecca found herself unable to move. "How could you do this?" she demanded. "Either of you?"

Steve's boyish face broke into an apologetic grin. In any other situation, she would have found it appealing. "Honey, you know, we hadn't actually done the deed, you and I, and we're not married yet. So, in a sense, it's not as if I'm cheating on you."

"Two hours before our wedding?" To her humiliation, her voice cracked.

"If I'd known you'd get so upset, I wouldn't have done it," he said in a placating tone that she'd heard before. Those times, it had worked. But those times, it had been used to smooth over some minor disagreement, not to belittle the destruction of her hopes and dreams.

She'd saved her virginity as a gift for her future husband, and he placed no importance at all on his own fidelity? Rebecca knew she couldn't respond without bursting into tears, so she focused on Esther instead. "What about you? What's your excuse?"

Her old friend tossed her head defiantly. "I don't need an excuse. I deserve him. You were always the one who got everything. Well, it's my turn."

"I was the one who got everything?" Rebecca repeated, stunned.

"You always had prettier clothes," her former friend whined. "And when you won that college scholarship, you were so happy to be going to Madison, you never even thought about me."

"I had more because I earned it." She'd worked after school and on weekends to pay for those clothes, and studied in the evenings while

Esther was watching TV. Until now, Rebecca hadn't had a clue her friend was nursing such petty jealousy.

"Whoa!" Steve held up his hands as if to stop a fight. He still showed no sign of discomfort at his nudity. "Let's not fight old battles, shall we? Rebecca, let's just chalk this up to the groom's last-minute jitters. Our friends and relatives will be arriving any minute. We don't need to make a public spectacle of our private disagreements."

"You can't expect me to marry you now!" she gasped.

"How will it look if you cancel on me at the last minute?" he said. "Besides, my feelings about you haven't changed, honey."

Esther smacked his shoulder. "You said you were in love with me! You said you needed a well-educated wife for business reasons!"

Rebecca's knees felt like rubber and her head hurt. She couldn't stand to be in the same room with these people for another second. "Goodbye, both of you."

"What will we tell the guests?" For the first time, Steve showed signs of agitation. "And my business clients? A wedding isn't merely a social occasion, it's a time to show your best side to the world!''

"It isn't a business *or* a social occasion!'' Rebecca flared. "It's a sacred pact between two people to devote their lives to each other. Esther, you're right. You deserve him.''

Dogged by a sense of unreality, she spun and left. The last thing she noticed was her clipboard sitting on a table next to the bed. But she wouldn't be needing it now.

In the wedding suite, Rebecca threw a few toiletry items into the suitcase she'd packed for the honeymoon, and tossed a coat over her shoulders. She couldn't even bear to take the time to change clothes.

Everything she saw carried painful associations. The suitcase was filled with new outfits and sexy lingerie that she'd planned to wear for Steve. There was a stack of thank-you notes with stamped envelopes, too, that Rebecca had imagined herself gleefully filling during a few spare moments. What would she tell people now?

She had to get away and sort through these overwhelming emotions. There was anger. Shame at having trusted two such unworthy people. Embarrassment at discovering that Steve thought so little of her. Above all, a deep-down sense of betrayal. How could she ever trust anyone again?

Rebecca didn't want to see anyone, but she couldn't leave without making some explanation to her mother. After that, she needed to find a hideout where she could cry and rage uninterrupted until she came to terms with what had happened.

In the lobby, she nearly collided with Diane, the photographer and a couple of guests. One look at her face and suitcase, and everyone but her mother withdrew discreetly.

If only the entire hotel would just fade away. If only today were already yesterday, or ten years ago.

"You can't be doing what I think you're doing," her mother said in a low voice.

"I caught them!" Rebecca forced back a sob. "Steve and Esther!"

"It has to be a misunderstanding." Her mom touched her arm reassuringly. "Were they kissing? I'm sure it was a brotherly thing."

"They were way beyond kissing!" Rebecca didn't care who heard her. That included Rick, who was approaching with a worried expression.

Of all people, she couldn't bear for him to witness her disgrace. Or what felt like disgrace, even if it wasn't her fault.

But her mother was summoning him over. Apparently, she'd decided he might make a good ally. "Rick, tell her Steve and Esther wouldn't do anything wrong."

"I saw them together!" Rebecca said between gritted teeth. She couldn't bring herself to give a more graphic description. The sight had been too painful.

"How about if I mash him into the woodwork?" Rick's response nearly made her smile, until he caught Diane's glare and abruptly amended his position. "I mean, maybe there's some other explanation. It is a little hard to believe."

"Even you don't understand, and I thought you were my best friend!" Becky cried, and, grasping her long skirt in one hand, rushed outside.

The limousine stood by the curb. As she flung herself inside, she realized where she wanted to go, a place that she could be utterly alone.

After all, who would think to look for a runaway bride in a honeymoon hotel?

CHAPTER TWO

THIS WEEKEND WAS turning out to be one of the more interesting ones since he joined his wife Molly in running the Breakfast Inn Bed, Quinn Spencer mused as he sat in the office just behind the reception desk.

Some interesting romances were developing among the current guests. And, as Molly had remarked this morning, there was nothing more satisfying than welcoming a pair of newlyweds to the Double Wedding Ring room.

"Is she here yet?" Four-year-old Sara peered into the office, regarding him hopefully from beneath her long blond bangs. "I want to see the bride!"

"Sara!" Molly came to tug gently on her daughter's hand. "Quinn's working on the books."

He glanced guiltily at the computer screen in front of him. It did indeed show the B&B's accounting program, but he'd been woolgathering, not entering the receipts.

"It's okay," he said. "This is a family enterprise, after all. Sara's part of the operation."

Molly smiled fondly. He knew she appreciated how quickly he'd bonded with his new stepdaughter. In fact, it had been easier than Quinn could have imagined.

He hoped the couples staying here would find an equal measure of happiness. Especially the honeymooners.

"I love seeing brides, too," Molly admitted. "I'll tell you what, Sara. Let's go in the living room. We can read *The Runaway Bunny* while we watch for—what are their names?"

"Mr. and Mrs. Whittman," Quinn replied.

"Okay," the little girl said brightly.

He'd barely returned to his bookkeeping when, from the living room, Molly called, "The limo's here! Don't get up, Quinn. I'll check them in."

No way was he going to miss the sight of the newcomers. Of course, brides usually changed into traveling clothes after the reception, but once in a while someone chose to stay in her finery and arrived looking like a fairy-tale princess. Quinn had never known he was such a romantic, until he got married and started running a bed and breakfast.

The front door of the Victorian home opened, revealing a blur of white and, in the background, a road-spattered limousine. Then the door shut abruptly.

She was alone. Alone, still in her wedding dress, and tear-streaked. Quinn's heart twisted in sympathy. But perhaps the newlyweds, overwrought by the day's events, had merely had a minor quarrel and would soon patch it up.

Molly, always the practical one, was ready with the key and the sign-in book. Moving briskly toward their red-haired guest, she said, "Hi, I'm Molly Spencer and this is my husband, Quinn. Welcome to Breakfast Inn Bed."

"Th-thank you." The woman scribbled in the book and took the key.

"It's upstairs, to the right." Molly gave a discreet cough. "When might we expect the groom?"

"When hell freezes over!" cried the bride and, clutching her suitcase, rushed upstairs.

Molly studied her signature. "Rebecca Salber. I guess she isn't Mrs. Whittman yet."

"Isn't her husband coming?" Sara asked.

"I'm sure he'll be along." Quinn gave her a reassuring hug. "It looks like they might have had a lovers' quarrel. If we're patient, we might even get to see the happy ending for ourselves."

UNDER ANY OTHER circumstances, Rebecca would have been charmed. The wintry landscape on the short drive to Tyler had been picture-postcard quaint, with barns and farmhouses silhouetted against the rolling hills. As for the town itself, it was exactly as Rick had described it.

The open central square, the brick town hall, even the names of the stores had a small-town coziness. And the green and white Victorian inn was right out of her girlhood daydreams.

But the dreams ended at the front door, when she had to enter all by herself. Rebecca had noticed how the little girl in the hall stared at her in dismay, as if Cinderella had fallen into a mud puddle. Which was exactly how Rebecca felt.

The handsome prince had proved to be nothing but a knave. As for the princess, she would soon return to her empty apartment, without even a dream left to cheer her up.

Inside her room, Rebecca dropped the suitcase

on a chair and flung herself across the bed. The quilt, she noticed dimly, was hand-stitched with a double ring pattern. Rick had mentioned that all the rooms were named after quilt designs.

She wondered if there was one labeled Broken Heart. Or, perhaps, Utterly Disgusted.

The tears that she'd struggled against in the limousine now spilled down Rebecca's cheeks unchecked. If only she could shut out the image of Steve sitting there in bed, unabashedly naked, and of Esther, gloating.

It didn't help to remember that she'd left her mother the painful task of making excuses to the guests. And Rebecca wished she hadn't snapped at Rick, either. None of this was his fault.

So, what as she going to do now? The wedding had cost a fortune, but that wasn't the main problem. It was her future. A trackless void loomed in place of the steady course she'd set for herself.

Rebecca rolled over on her back to keep her tears from dampening the quilt. How could she have made such a mistake in the man she'd chosen?

She'd been so careful, all her life. Early on, Rebecca had determined never to get left in the lurch as her mother had, nor to be forced to work her way up from the bottom. It had taken decades for Diane, who had started out waiting tables, to reach an executive position at Swan's Folly.

That was why Rebecca had studied so hard and worked long hours in high school. That was part of the reason, along with a love for numbers, that she'd chosen accounting as her profession.

When it came to men, she'd dated plenty of them and said no to them all. No, she wasn't going to jump into bed and risk a pregnancy. No, she refused to get married until she found Mr. Right, and double-checked his references for good measure.

She'd met Steve ten months ago when he came to her accounting firm to troubleshoot a new computer system. His easy sense of humor and good manners had made him immediately popular, but he'd had eyes only for Rebecca.

Or so she'd believed. Now she tortured herself with doubts. How had he behaved when they weren't together? Maybe he'd had other girlfriends all along.

She couldn't help doubting everything about

him. On their dates, he'd usually taken her to business-related social events, rarely suggesting a quiet evening together. At the time, she'd been grateful that he wasn't trying to get her into bed. Now she wondered if, as Esther had indicated, he'd mostly valued her for the professional demeanor and sharp wardrobe that impressed his clients.

Not that she cared. In fact, she ought to be congratulating herself on her narrow escape.

Why did she still feel so rotten?

MOLLY HANDED QUINN a cup of hot chocolate. "It's almost dark. I hope he gets here soon."

He checked his watch. The bride had been here for half an hour. "I bet he'll show up any minute."

"Will they get married here?" Sara asked eagerly. "Can I watch?"

Quinn chuckled. "We've never had a wedding at the Breakfast Inn Bed, but that doesn't mean we couldn't start a new tradition."

"On a weekend?" Molly asked. "I'd like to know where we'd find the minister. But just think! They could tie the knot on Valentine's Day."

It was fun to speculate. Not that the Spencers really expected to see their guests' wedding first-hand, but at the Breakfast Inn Bed, every day seemed like an adventure.

When the front door opened a few minutes later, Quinn found himself grinning. Just as he'd expected, here was the groom, handsomely attired in a black and white tuxedo beneath his open coat.

Wait a minute. That wasn't some guy named Steve Whittman. It was Ricky Travis, former star quarterback for the Tyler Titans. He'd been two years behind Quinn in high school.

According to the town grapevine, Ricky had excelled in college football and played pro ball before an elbow injury ended his career. Some gossips had contended he would sink into self-pity, but instead he'd parlayed a marketing degree into a successful career in advertising.

Molly, however, hadn't grown up in Tyler and didn't recognize him. She stepped forward, guest book in hand. "Hi! We've been expecting you."

Ricky, better known as Rick these days, brushed a fleck of dirt off his coat. "You have?"

"He isn't the groom," Quinn said. Molly shot

him a dubious look. "That's Rick Travis. He's from around here."

"Where's Becky?" Rick asked. "She's here, isn't she?"

"Upstairs to the right in the Double Wedding Ring," Quinn said. "What's going on, if you don't mind my asking?"

"There's been a change of plans," Rick replied, and marched up the stairs.

"Why is that man wearing a tuxedo if he isn't the groom?" Molly asked, as if Quinn might actually know the answer.

"Maybe he's a bridesmaid," said Sara.

"Don't be silly." Her mother chuckled. "He must be the best man."

"A better man than the groom, if Mr. Whittman doesn't get his act in here fast," muttered Quinn.

RICK WAS ALMOST SORRY he'd figured out where Becky was hiding. If she didn't want to marry Steve, she shouldn't do it.

On the other hand, he couldn't help sympathizing with Diane's distress. It had taken guts for her to stand there at the entrance to the ballroom, telling the arriving guests that the bride and groom were having a disagreement. "I'm sure it will be cleared up, but if they're not one hundred percent sure, they shouldn't go ahead with the wedding," she'd said. Then she'd directed everyone into the reception room to enjoy dinner and dancing.

Privately, she'd told Rick, "I'm sure she's overreacting. Maybe Esther volunteered to help Steve get dressed. Some guys are all thumbs when it comes to putting on a tuxedo. Rebecca must have seen them and assumed the worst."

Rick found that scenario unlikely. Still, it was hard to imagine that any man would stoop to doing what she'd accused Steve of.

At Diane's insistence, the guests were still enjoying the refreshments and the band, and probably would be for another hour or so. There was time for the show to go on, so to speak, and the mother of the bride had begged Rick to make the short drive to Tyler to fetch her daughter.

He'd been reluctant, yet he could hardly refuse Diane's request point-blank. At least he could make the effort, he'd decided.

He just hoped his good deed wouldn't backfire. Rick didn't want to spoil a beautiful friendship by antagonizing Becky.

Heck, the whole reason he'd been such a good sport about this man-of-honor business, and about her marrying a shallow guy like Steve, was that he didn't want to ruin the best relationship of his life. Girlfriends came and went. Becky was his pal, his confidante, his comrade in arms against life's vicissitudes. Of course, they fought a lot too, but that was because they were equally strong-willed.

So Rick didn't put much stock in his chances of taking her back to Lake Geneva. But he'd promised to try, and here he was.

He knocked several times before footsteps indicated someone was coming. Then the door opened.

There stood Becky, eyes puffy, cheeks tear-streaked, red hair wisping free of its upsweep. Her white dress was rumpled.

Even in this disarrayed state, she looked cute. Rick experienced an urge to protect her, which he immediately suppressed. Despite her small size, Becky was plenty capable of taking care of herself.

"Rick?" She blinked a couple of times. "I should have guessed you'd be the one to find me." She stood back and let him inside.

"You look terrible," he said.

"Gee, thanks."

"I mean, you look like you feel terrible," he amended. On the bed, the quilt was bunched where she'd been lying there, weeping. "Your mom's worried."

"Is she all right?" Becky wiped a tear on her sleeve, then regarded the smeared fabric in dismay. "I shouldn't have done that."

"I'm sure we can get you properly fluffed up," Rick said. "Your mom's hoping you'll come back. There's still time to pull this thing off."

Her eyes narrowed until the sheen of moisture glittered dangerously. "Is that why you came here, to patch things up between me and Steve?"

"Whoa!" Rick held up his hands in mock defensiveness. "I'm just your mother's messenger. But let's look at the situation objectively, Beck. Item one, you agree to marry this guy. You dazzle us all with an engagement ring as bright as a supernova, which you're still wearing, by the way."

Startled, she tugged at the heavy ring with its large diamond surrounded by a swirl of smaller stones. It stuck on her finger. "I can't get it off."

"Is that heavy symbolism or what?" he teased.

"I'll use olive oil. Whatever they've got in the kitchen."

"Hold on. I'm not finished," he said. "Item two, you and your mom spend the U.S. mint on a wedding. Item three, you invite the entire known world to descend on Lake Geneva, plus I had to rent this tux. Not that I'm asking for a refund. Just making a point."

"You think I'm obligated to go through with the ceremony to fulfill other people's expectations? Or because we've spent money on it?" Becky asked in disbelief. "What about Steve? What does he have to say for himself?"

"He was pretty upset." It sounded weak, even to Rick. If he'd had his way, he would have dragged the groom here by the ears to make him face the music, but Diane didn't believe the man could persuade her daughter as well as Rick could.

"Then why didn't he come with you?"

"He said he was being slandered in front of his friends and business associates and needed to smooth their ruffled feathers. But—these are his words, not mine—he loves you and he's devastated about what happened.'' The guy was a less than credible actor, in Rick's opinion, but he'd been sent as a go-between, not a theater critic.

"Has he admitted what happened?" Becky demanded.

"He claims it was a misunderstanding."

She got very, very quiet. Rick had to fight the urge to make a quick exit, because he knew the volcanic explosion was only moments away.

Becky didn't erupt, though, not the way she'd done the time he was half an hour late for the ballet and they missed the opening pas de deux. Instead, she spoke with a tension that underscored the depth of her anger.

"Regardless of what you may think, I'm not an idiot," she said. "I saw them. In Esther's bed. Undressed. All relevant body parts on deck. Got it?"

He was shocked. Dismayed. Intrigued. "You could actually see...?"

She nodded.

"He couldn't have tripped and...?"

She shook her head.

Rick had heard the expression, "seeing red," but he'd never experienced it before. Now, he felt as if someone had waved a red flag in his face, transforming him into an enraged bull. "That dirty low-down excuse for a human being had the nerve to say he was being slandered! He called you hysterical."

"I probably was hysterical," she admitted.

He pictured Steve, standing in the hotel lobby with his face a mask of wounded innocence. People had gathered around making sympathetic noises, and the man had egged them on with his display of long-suffering patience. As if he were the injured party. As if Becky were guilty of some offense.

"Someone needs to teach that creep a lesson." Rick's primitive masculine instincts, untamed despite thousands of years of more or less civilized ancestors, were fully aroused. "You shouldn't be the only one crying tonight, Beck." His hands clenching into fists, he started for the door.

"Wait!" She caught his arm. "You're not going to beat him up, are you?"

Rick hadn't thought beyond possibly pitching

Steve into the punch bowl. "I'll confront him with the truth and let nature take its course."

"No!" Becky hung on. "You can't go!"

"Why not?" The adrenaline was pumping. Rick wondered if he dared risk supersonic speeds en route to the hotel. Maybe he wouldn't even need a car.

"For one thing, you'll ruin what's left of my mother's evening," Becky said. "And you might get arrested. Besides, you have to stay here."

The red haze in Rick's brain lifted slightly. "Why?"

"Because I don't want to be alone." Her mouth quivered, and a drop of moisture spilled down her cheek. "I don't know anyone else I can turn to. Even my mom would just give me a lecture about how I've let people down."

"I promise not to give you any more lectures." Rick folded himself into an armchair and, without thinking, gathered Becky onto his lap. "It's fine with me if you don't get married. We can have lunch like we always do. There's a couple of good movies coming out, too."

She curled against him. For all her feistiness, the woman was cuddly as a kitten. "They

wouldn't happen to be romantic comedies?''
That was her favorite type of film.

"No," he admitted, inhaling the jasmine-
scented freshness of her hair. "Science fiction,
the good kind with monsters."

"Okay." She nuzzled his neck. "If you'll go
to the ice show with me."

"It's a deal." They should have tried sitting
this way before, with their arms wound around
each other and their faces close together. It felt
wonderfully relaxing after the stress of the last
few hours.

At least, it felt relaxing for a few minutes.
Then Rick started getting tense in a different
way.

Becky's emotional sharp edges were offset by
soft physical curves. He'd noticed them before,
in an objective sort of way. But their contact had
always been limited to accidental touching and,
occasionally, linking arms when they attended
an event together.

Never before had her head rested on his shoulder, or her full breasts pressed against his chest.
From this angle, he couldn't help noticing the
enticing way her neckline dipped.

Whoever designed this wedding gown must

have intentionally made it sexy. Nothing else could explain the tautness that seized Rick as he noticed the valley of Becky's cleavage, with no sign of a restricting brassiere.

He didn't intend to behave rashly, but one kiss wouldn't do any harm. Her lips were so close, and parted so invitingly.

With his arm around her back, he lifted her against him. She offered no resistance as Rick bent to claim her mouth.

REBECCA HAD OBSERVED the first time they met that Rick was an incredibly sexy man. From time to time, she'd even allowed herself to fantasize about being gripped in his arms and held tight against his powerful body.

Then she'd learned how easily he changed girlfriends and how careless he could be about keeping commitments. She'd resolved to be platonic friends ever since.

Tonight, though, she needed someone to fill the hollow where her husband should have been. It was more an emotional need than a physical one, and yet the longer Rick held her, the more her body responded.

He was gentle but thorough. As he kissed her, she felt surrounded and sheltered.

Rebecca didn't want to fight anymore. She was tired of keeping up barriers. For once, she simply went with her feelings.

Wonderful silver sensations rippled across her skin as he lightly chafed her upper arms with his hands. "Cold?" Rick murmured.

"Getting warmer," she said.

"I could build a fire." He nodded toward the fireplace, where logs and kindling had been set in place.

"You already are," she said.

Rick looked as contented as a cat. He was a beautiful man, she admitted silently, with that dramatic dark hair and those bright blue eyes.

Reaching up, he plucked the hairpins from her French twist. Soft curls cascaded around her shoulders. "Now you're the Becky I know."

"I thought it would be fun being a bride." She sighed. "It was awful."

"I like your dress, though." He traced one finger along the neckline, across the edges of her breasts. "It's sexy."

Rebecca's nipples sprang erect, and now she really *was* hot. This was as far as she'd ever let a man go, even Steve, and she'd never responded this strongly before.

Rick's chest heaved faster as he eased down the shoulders of her gown, exposing more cleavage. She hadn't worn a bra, afraid that a strap might show during the wedding, and that fact was immediately obvious.

He shifted her into a reclining position, and lowered her gown even more. His moist breath tickled across her exposed breast, and then his lips seized the nipple.

Rebecca gasped and clung to Rick. Her entire body riveted on that one point of flame.

As he bared the other breast, she hoped...she needed...yes, there it was, his mouth on that aching tip, moving back and forth between the two, and then to her mouth again.

His tongue quested, and hers responded. Her body moved with rhythms she'd never before known, in a dance that she could only share with Rick.

Through the haze of sexual desire, Rebecca's common sense intruded. What were they doing? What could she be thinking?

She was practically throwing herself at her best friend. If she didn't call a halt, they might never be able to look each other in the eye again.

"Wait!" she rasped. "Please!"

Rick stopped abruptly. His ragged breathing was the only sound she heard.

Embarrassed, Rebecca yanked up the front of her dress. "I don't know what came over me."

Rick's hooded expression gave no clue to his reaction. "Getting Steve out of your system, I expect."

Steve hadn't even entered her mind. It was Rick she'd wanted, but she must have been crazy. "Temporary insanity is more like it." She untangled herself and stood up stiffly.

"I didn't mean to take advantage," he said. "Honest, my motives were pure. I came here to cheer you up and maybe save the wedding."

"By seducing the bride?" Rebecca challenged as she smoothed her skirt.

"I was reminding you that you're a desirable woman," he said.

If he meant that as a compliment, it failed utterly. His cavalier tone spoke louder than his words.

He'd been fooling around, something he'd probably done a hundred times with as many different women. Rebecca meant no more to him than they had.

It had hurt badly enough to discover that

Steve didn't love her. Rick's offhand way of reminding her that she wasn't special to him felt like a knife in the ribs.

Rebecca wasn't about to confess that she'd never shared that much of herself with another man before. Or that Rick had stirred a response she hadn't known she was capable of. No matter what storm raged inside her, she had to maintain a calm appearance.

"Let's do ourselves a favor and pretend it never happened," she said.

Someone tapped on the door. Rebecca's heart sank. She hoped it wasn't her mother. Or, worse, Steve, especially when she felt so vulnerable.

After checking to make sure her dress was straight, she opened the door. Molly Spencer held out a small brightly wrapped package. "This just came for you. With Valentine's Day so close, we've been receiving deliveries at all hours."

"Thanks." Puzzled, Rebecca took the gift. It weighed hardly anything.

To her credit, the innkeeper didn't peer inside or ask foolish questions about whether Rebecca was having a good time. She simply smiled and went away.

"Go on, open it." Rick strolled toward Rebecca. "I'm dying to know what's inside."

If it was from Steve, she wouldn't accept it. However, in the absence of any attached note, she had to open the gift to find out who had sent it.

As was her habit, Rebecca peeled off the ribbon carefully and lifted away the paper virtually undamaged. Inside lay a white cardboard box about the right size for lacy lingerie.

Rick peered over her shoulder as she lifted the lid. Atop the folded tissue paper lay an unsigned card bearing the name and address of a novelty gift shop in Lake Geneva. The message read, "From a man who desires you."

"Are you going to take all day to open it? I'm dying of curiosity." Rick reached over and snatched something bright red from beneath the tissue paper.

"Hey!" she protested.

"What the—?" Open-mouthed, he dangled the thing in midair. It was a scarlet fake-fur bikini top.

From the box, Rebecca lifted a matching bikini bottom. "This has to be the tackiest thing I've ever seen."

"I think it's kind of sweet," Rick said in a fake falsetto. In his own voice, he added, "Come on, Beck, it's a gag gift that a groom ordered for his wedding night. Goofy, but affectionate, too."

She was too tired to argue. And too overwhelmed by a rush of unwanted emotions. As he'd reminded her, this was supposed to be her wedding night.

"I don't care who sent it. It's ugly." Whipping the top from his hands, Rebecca threw the bikini and box into the closet. "You should go home now. Or back to the hotel, if you insist, and make your excuses to my mother."

All hint of laughter faded from his face. "I'll call her. There's no point in driving back, and if I do, I might remember I'm your friend and pop Steve in the kisser."

"Good night." Rebecca stayed clear of the doorway, to preclude any possibility of a farewell hug. She didn't trust herself around Rick, not tonight.

After he left, she leaned against the inside of the door and reflected that this had been the absolutely worst day of her life. She'd humiliated her mother, inconvenienced her guests, been betrayed by the man she thought she loved...

And, worst of all, she'd nearly abandoned herself to Rick's embrace, only to discover that he cared no more for her than for any of those women he'd dated over the years.

Fighting back a surge of tears, she went to take a hot shower and soap off her engagement ring.

CHAPTER THREE

BELLS ECHOED FROM the Methodist church two blocks away as Rick jogged around the Tyler town square. He'd gone to an early service at the Fellowship Lutheran Church, then changed clothes and headed outside to work off energy after a restless night.

The air was almost too chilly for running, even with a heavy jacket and gloves, but he needed the exercise. Otherwise, he might explode like a skyrocket.

Besides, Rick didn't intend to let himself get soft. The weakness in his elbow might preclude a sports career. It didn't require him to turn into a couch potato.

His running shoes smacked against the sidewalk as he passed Gates Department Store. In the display window, a mannequin in a designer suit regarded him coldly.

What the heck had he been thinking when he

took Becky onto his lap last night? Rick wondered. He'd gone there to comfort her.

His response had been alarming. Not so much because he wanted sex, which for a twenty-eight-year-old guy was pretty much a given, but because he'd wanted it with Becky.

Of all the women he'd ever met, she was the only one who had the potential to make him miserable. If he ever allowed himself to fall in love with that sharp-witted, bossy, opinionated, endearing lady, she would turn his life upside-down and remodel him in her own image.

He liked her the way she was. And he liked himself the way he was, too. Most of the time.

Rick cut across the square beneath skeletal trees that, in summer, would provide shade for the townspeople as they ate lunch on the benches, flirted with their sweethearts and attended special events. He missed the people and the flowers that usually lined the walkways.

The thought of flowers reminded him that tomorrow was Valentine's Day. If he were Becky's boyfriend, he wouldn't have bought her a ridiculous red bikini. He'd have sent a dozen roses and a big box of chocolate candy, most of which he'd have eaten himself.

Okay, so there was a method to his madness. Becky would understand.

He started getting mad at Steve again for hurting her. And a little irked at Becky for picking that jerk when she could have had someone more worthwhile. Someone more like Rick.

He no longer doubted that Becky had seen what she thought she'd seen occurring between her fiancé and her bridesmaid. If Steve were innocent, he'd have grilled Rick and Diane until he found out where his bride had gone, and then he'd have come after her.

It was hard to understand a guy like that. True, Rick played the field, dodging numerous attempts to pin him down. But he never intentionally misled a woman about where she stood with him.

And if he were engaged to Becky—which, of course, he would never be, but supposing he were in some alternate lifetime—he couldn't imagine cheating on her. It was rotten. It was incomprehensible. How could Steve even be tempted?

The steady pounding of his thighs and calves, along with the ache in his lungs, finally eased Rick's anger. It also helped to reflect that Becky was lucky she'd discovered the truth about that creep before the wedding.

Leaving the town square, Rick jogged past the Tyler Savings and Loan and along Main Street one block to Gunther, where he turned right. A flew blocks later, he arrived at the wood-frame home he'd bought with the earnings from his abbreviated football career.

Rick's friends from the ad agency had urged him to rent an apartment in Madison so he could be close to the action. And sometimes he did crash on a pal's couch when the evening's activities ran late.

But Tyler was home. As he unlocked the door, Rick smiled in anticipation. He loved having his own place right in town, after having grown up on a farm.

He stepped inside and paused to scan the old-fashioned furniture and the landscape photographs that reflected the unique vision of fellow townsman Byron Forrester. Rick spared a particularly fond glance for the upright piano where he practiced whenever he got a chance, although it was years since he'd taken a lesson from Nora Gates Forrester.

It wasn't the sort of place where Becky Salber

would want to live, he mused as he headed for the bedroom. Her tastes were more modern. She would choose an airy house with sleek furnishings and abstract artwork. Of course, it would be located in Madison so she could shop at trendy boutiques and catch the latest movies, too.

She was a big-city girl, while he loved small-town life. He looked forward to camping and backpacking, while Becky had once admitted that, to her, "roughing it" meant a motor home with a bathroom.

As he stripped off his exercise clothes, Rick's heart twinged. Why did they have to be so different?

Well, they were, and it couldn't be changed. He enjoyed her quick mind and warm heart, but they disagreed about almost everything.

As friends, they were great. As lovers, they would be a complete mismatch.

"STEVE MISSES YOU TERRIBLY. He hasn't left the hotel, you know." Over the phone, Diane's voice hovered between concern for the groom and reproof for her daughter. "He swears you misunderstood everything."

It was on the tip of Rebecca's tongue to demand that he tell her so himself, when she remembered that she didn't want to talk to him.

"Look, Mom, I'm really sorry about what I've put you through and I'll pay you back every penny." She'd said that before, but it bore repeating. "However, if he's hanging around Lake Geneva, it's probably so he can spend more time with Esther."

When her mother didn't answer right away, Rebecca knew she'd hit a nerve. Finally Diane said, "Esther's been here, too, but only because she wants me to know how bad she feels about what happened. I mean, about what you *think* happened."

Why did Diane refuse to believe her own daughter? Why didn't she give Rebecca, rather than Steve, the benefit of the doubt?

It would be easy to throw those questions at her mother, but it would be useless. Rebecca knew why Diane was bending over backwards for her worthless almost-son-in-law.

She'd seen for herself, over the years, the contradiction in her mother's character. At work, Diane was decisive, independent-minded and thorough. When it came to men, though, she had a large blind spot.

Any charming scoundrel could wrap her around his little finger. After the divorce, there'd been a series of other disastrous relationships. Rebecca had resigned herself to picking up the pieces, and listening to her mother's self-recriminations when she finally saw the truth, after the damage was done.

Diane identified so strongly with her daughter that she'd applied her blind spot to Steve. He was another silver-tongued rogue, just as Rebecca's father had been.

The thing that galled her most was that she hadn't seen it, either. Only a chance visit to Esther's room had torn the veil, literally and figuratively, from her eyes.

"I'm not coming back," she said, to cut off further pleas on Steve and Esther's behalf. "I know what they did, and they know what they did. Whether you believe me or not, Mom, nothing's going to change."

"We'll talk about this again later," her mother said tightly. "I hope you do some deep thinking, Rebecca."

"Yes, I will. Bye, Mom. I love you." She

hung up and gazed around the snug room. Framed quilted squares in a variety of patterns hung on the walls, and bright rugs softened the polished hardwood floor. The caring touches made Rebecca feel a little better.

She decided to count her blessings. She'd never slept with Steve. Nor had she given up her job, although the lease on her apartment ran out in two weeks and another renter had already signed on. Maybe she could move in with a friend until she found a new one.

Her best friend was Rick, she remembered with a start, but she couldn't move in with him! Not after what had happened last night.

Rebecca sank into the padded chair. It was right here that he'd held her, his blue eyes shining so close to hers. She'd never dreamed they could arouse such passion in each other.

A Stop sign flashed in her brain. Rick was a red-blooded American male. Any halfway attractive woman could raise him to a white heat, at least temporarily.

She was not going to sit here in her robe and worry about things, Rebecca decided. She'd eaten breakfast on a tray, which meant she hadn't seen much of the inn beyond the entrance hall. Although she didn't feel up to venturing outdoors, she wouldn't mind exploring the common rooms she'd studied in the brochure.

Before she did anything else, she decided to unpack. Last night, she hadn't wanted to bother, but now she could almost hear the clothes wrinkling inside her suitcase.

Rebecca set to work. Unfortunately, as she lifted out each garment and arranged it on a hanger, unwanted memories stirred.

This tailored green suit, for instance. She had pictured herself wearing it when she and Steve went out to eat. As for the slinky cocktail dress with the spaghetti straps begging for a man to slide them down her arms, it didn't bear thinking about.

Rebecca decided to wear brown wool slacks and a tan fisherman's sweater. At least she'd had no specific plans for this outfit.

A short time later, dressed and sporting a pair of walking shoes, she ventured into the second-floor hallway, which was lined by five rooms. Although steps led up to a third level, a small sign indicated these were private family quarters, so she headed down instead.

On the lower level, Rebecca hesitated. The

male innkeeper stood at the small reception desk, making a notation on a ledger. There was no reason for him to object to her exploring his house, yet she wondered if she would be intruding.

She searched her memory for his name, and dredged it up. "Good morning, Quinn."

The tall man gave her a friendly smile. "Good morning. Can I help you with something?"

"Is it all right if I poke around?" she asked. "I'm curious to see the rest of the house."

"The downstairs rooms are all public," he said. "I'd be happy to serve as your guide, if you'd like."

To Rebecca's surprise, she realized that she would enjoy talking to someone. Nevertheless, she said, "I wouldn't want to intrude. After all, it is Sunday."

"We never take a day off," he replied. "Besides, I enjoy getting to know people. It's something that surprised me about this business."

"Really? How did you get into it?"

"My wife inherited this house from her first husband." After setting down his pen, Quinn led the way across the front hall. "She's the one who converted it to a bed and breakfast. I married into the business."

"Lucky man," Rebecca said.

"Very lucky." In the living room, he pointed out the fireplace and the Victorian-style sofas and chairs. "Our guests are welcome to use this room whenever they like. Some people prefer the privacy of their rooms, but others enjoy socializing."

"It's enchanting." Until now, Rebecca had always preferred spare modern furnishings. Like numbers and accounting systems, they projected a sense of order.

Yet, since arriving at the Breakfast Inn Bed, she'd found she enjoyed knowing that someone had hand-stitched the quilts and that this old furniture had a history, a place in people's lives.

Quinn showed her the book- and game-filled library at the back of the house, then the formal dining room and the large, well-appointed kitchen. No one else was around, so his wife and daughter must be upstairs, Rebecca thought.

"How about a cup of hot chocolate?" he asked. "There's nothing more relaxing than a cup of cocoa savored in the library."

"That would be great." As he moved about

preparing the beverage, Rebecca discovered a deep need to talk to someone objective. Particularly a male someone.

Her mother's scolding still buzzed in her ears. Even Rick hadn't been as harsh on Steve last night as she would have expected. Rebecca didn't believe she was being unfair, but, with her usual thoroughness, she wanted to eliminate any doubt.

"I guess you're wondering why I abandoned my groom," she said.

"I try not to be nosy," Quinn replied affably as he poured the steaming chocolate into two mugs.

"Maybe you can give me some insight," Rebecca said. "Do you mind if I use you as a sounding board?"

"Sound away," he said.

"I caught him cheating on me with one of the bridesmaids. My mother thinks I should go ahead with the wedding. Even my best friend tried to talk me into it, and he's a guy himself."

The innkeeper carried the cups out of the kitchen, and Rebecca followed. When they were settled in the library, Quinn stretched out his long legs and said, "If I may be blunt..."

"Please do."

"This groom of yours sounds like bad news." He shook his head. "Why does your mother want you to marry him?"

"She doesn't believe I saw what I saw, or she doesn't choose to," Rebecca said. "Steve's an impressive guy. He's got an up-and-coming business and he's trying to establish a position in society. The way he curries important acquaintances, maybe he even wants to run for office someday."

"I suppose a lot of people would consider that impressive," Quinn agreed.

"But I can't forgive him," she said. "What's more, I'm sure that, if he'd cheat on me once, he'll do it again."

The innkeeper met her gaze over the foam on his chocolate. "If you're looking for confirmation from me, you've got it. Nobody should get married unless they're absolutely certain it's the right thing to do."

Buoyed by his support, Rebecca felt free to explore her own mixed feelings. "My dad abandoned Mom and me for another woman when I was young. But maybe it's not fair to put Steve in the same category. We weren't actually married yet, and we...hadn't been intimate. So he claimed he wasn't betraying me.''

"Let's bend credibility and assume he's sincere about that," Quinn said. "If he was that attracted to another woman, or that unwilling to wait a few hours to keep faith with his wife, it means he isn't being honest with himself about wanting to marry you. My mother made that mistake, and it's caused no end of grief.''

Rebecca was instantly fascinated and sympathetic. "What happened?''

"My parents came from society families in New York." He set his cup on a coaster. "I think Dad was in love with Violet, but she must not have felt the same way. Nevertheless, she allowed herself to be pressured or persuaded into marrying him.''

"Was she in love with someone else?''

"Not then, I don't think," Quinn said. "But later, when I was a kid, she began having an affair with a man named Ray Bennedict. Dad's not an easygoing guy, as anyone in Tyler can tell you, but he valued his marriage enough to quit his job and move us all here. He thought the distance might enable him and Violet to make a fresh start.''

"Why do you call your mother by her first name?" Rebecca asked.

"Because I didn't grow up around her." He sounded sad. "Six months after we moved to Tyler, when I was seven, she left Dad. At first, she sought custody of my two brothers and me, but then she disappeared. She never even finalized the divorce."

"That's strange," Rebecca said. "Did you search for her?"

"Dad adamantly refused," Quinn said. "My brothers and I talked about hiring a detective, after we were grown, but we didn't want to upset my father. Or make him angry, either. He's an old-fashioned kind of guy."

"You must have wondered what happened to your mother."

Quinn's mouth twisted wryly. "I thought about her a lot. But I figured Mom simply didn't care about us, so I tried to let her go. Can you understand that?"

"Yes." There'd come a point when Rebecca had had to force herself to stop hoping for a close relationship with her own father. "I haven't seen or talked to my dad since before my high school graduation," she said. "He called and promised to attend, but he didn't. He never apologized or explained, either. It was kind of the last straw after a lifetime of disappointments.''

"In my case, it turns out there was a good reason why Violet never visited us," Quinn said. "My brothers and I learned recently by chance that she died in childbirth seven months after she left. Ray Bennedict is gone now, too. So we've got a half sibling somewhere that we're trying to find.''

"That *is* quite a story." Rebecca was glad he'd shared it with her.

"A family got torn apart because two people married who shouldn't have," Quinn concluded. "You asked for my opinion. Well, I'm one hundred percent in your camp.''

"Thanks. I just hope that I don't keep making the same mistake, by picking the wrong guy again next time," Rebecca admitted. "My mom has terrible judgment about men, and maybe I do, too. I honestly believed Steve would make a good husband. How could I be so blind as to think we had a terrific relationship?''

"Did you ever argue?" Quinn said.

"No, never.''

"That's a bad sign," he said. "People who care about each other don't avoid the tough issues. If you can't fight fair and then resolve your differences, you aren't really being open with each other."

Rebecca barely stopped herself from mentioning that she and Rick fought nearly all the time, and that wasn't so great, either. Somehow she didn't want to discuss Rick with anyone.

The front bell rang. Quinn uncoiled from his chair. "Duty calls."

"I'll take the mugs to the kitchen." Rebecca hurried to keep her word, then couldn't resist peeking into the front hall to say who'd arrived.

Quinn, holding a festively wrapped package, stood talking to a dark-haired man who sent her heart slamming into her chest. It was Rick, his coat open to reveal a blue plaid shirt tucked into faded jeans.

When he spotted her, he stopped talking abruptly, as if he'd lost track of the conversation. Then he gave her a smile that warmed her all over.

"The delivery service and I arrived at the same time," he said, indicating the package. "I wish I could claim I'd brought you that present. Or maybe not, depending on what it is.''

"I'm going to go help my wife fix lunch," Quinn said diplomatically, although Rebecca hadn't seen Molly come downstairs. "You two have a good time." Handing her the package, he strolled away.

"I'd better open it right away," Rebecca told Rick. "Otherwise we might both die of curiosity."

"You're not kidding, after what arrived yesterday."

He followed her into the living room. This time, Rebecca didn't bother to preserve the paper. She ripped into it, and pulled out a red fake-fur jock strap.

"Wow," Rick said, laughing. "Why didn't I think of sending you that?"

"At least it matches the bikini." Rebecca sighed. "Did I really almost marry a guy who has this kind of bad taste? You wouldn't know it from the expensive suits he wears."

"Maybe it's not from him," Rick said.

"Then who?"

"Are any of your friends fond of jokes?" he asked. "Aside from me, of course."

"I don't think so. I'd better check the card."
When she found it in the tissue paper, it was
from the same novelty gift shop. Aloud, she
read, "'I'll be coming to model this for you
soon.' No signature."

Rick shook his head in amazement. "I hope
this isn't Steve's way of trying to win you back.
If so, somebody ought to give him an award for
stupidity."

"We could call and ask the shopkeeper who
it's from." Rebecca fingered the card. "Do you
suppose a gift store would be open on a Sunday?"

"They had a delivery service working today,
and they're likely to be swamped because of
Valentine's Day tomorrow," Rick said. "It's
worth a try."

"Come with me." Rebecca had left her cell
phone in her room. "In case I giggle too hard
to talk, you'll need to take over."

"I wouldn't miss it!"

They crowded each other going up the stairs,
playfully jockeying for the lead. Some of Rebecca's tension melted. It was great to be pals
again with Rick, on a casual level that felt comfortable.

RICK LOVED SEEING Becky this way, her red hair tumbling around her shoulders and her green eyes sparkling with merriment. She was practically her old self again, right down to her ring-free left hand.

The problem, he conceded when they reached the suite, was that he wasn't sure he could forget what had happened between them last night. The contact had been intense enough to throw him off stride.

If she'd been anyone else, he'd have asked her on a date. In fact, a whole lot of dates. No sense in leaving any boring white spaces on her calendar for at least the next few months.

But she was treating him like her old friend, not like a man who'd aroused her to new heights of passion. Maybe they weren't new. Maybe she'd merely been working off steam to get Steve out of her system.

If so, Rick had only himself to blame for his behavior last night. He'd known she was vulnerable. Yet even now, his body buzzed at her nearness.

So, what else was new? With a bit of concentration, he knew how to bring his masculine instincts under control. All he had to do was imagine himself drinking vinegar. Or getting a traffic ticket.

Becky dialed the number on the gift card. A couple of rings later, someone answered.

She explained the situation. Rick could tell the person on the other end wasn't identifying the sender, even though Becky used her most persuasive manner.

"Thanks," she said at last, and ended the call.

"Well?" Rick, who was within arm's reach of her, mulled moving a little closer, or maybe a little further away. He'd never been so self-conscious around Becky before.

"The woman said she has strict orders not to reveal who ordered the gifts," she told him. "She did admit that the customer was in a big hurry when he came in on Friday and it's possible he gave her the wrong address."

"How could it be the wrong address? Your name was on the packages, and they reached you," Rick pointed out.

"That's true." Becky frowned. "It had to be Steve. Except, since he was going to be right here with me, why bother to hide the fact that he sent the gifts?"

"At least we know it's not an attempt to win

you back, since the gifts were ordered *before* the wedding,'' Rick muttered. There was no immediate way to clear up the mystery, and his stomach was sending hunger signals. ''How about lunch?''

''Sorry, I don't have a refrigerator you can raid,'' she said.

In Madison, he occasionally stopped by her apartment to make himself a sandwich after work when he had an evening meeting or a game to attend. ''I didn't mean that. Besides, I'd like to take you out for lunch at Tyler's finest.''

''Sunday brunch?'' she asked. ''All-you-can-eat delicacies with champagne?''

''Close enough,'' he said. ''Let's go.'' After all, he was sure she would find something she liked on the menu at Marge's Diner.

CHAPTER FOUR

REBECCA HAD BEEN dubious when Rick assured her that slacks and a sweater were suitable attire for brunch at Tyler's premier restaurant. She understood better when he parked his car in front of a café labeled Marge's Diner.

"This is the best restaurant in town?" she asked.

"Judging by the company, absolutely. Although some people would swear by the Old Heidelburg, it's not as much fun, in my book."

When he opened the front door, warm air scented with maple syrup, coffee and hamburgers lured Rebecca inside. A radio was playing country music, its rhythms punctuated by the clatter of dishes and the hum of conversation.

She was surprised to see so many people here at noontime on a Sunday. Most, she gathered from their suits and dresses, must have come after church.

Several people called greetings to Rick, whom they addressed as Ricky. He greeted them in return but didn't stop to chat.

Once the two of them were seated in a red vinyl booth, Rebecca ordered the blueberry pancakes and, for good measure, a slice of apple pie. Steve would have made some remark about watching her waistline. He always worried about making a good impression on others.

Rebecca hadn't minded, since she liked staying in control of herself with a strict diet and exercise program. But heck, she was an adult. If she chose to splurge once in a while, who needed to live with the weight police?

"A penny for your thoughts," Rick said.

She told him.

"Are you sure one slice of apple pie is enough?" Rick deadpanned.

Rebecca chuckled. "You have some wonderful qualities, much as I hate to admit it. If you weren't such a playboy, you might make some woman a terrific husband."

"You think I'm a playboy?" he asked. "What gave you that impression?"

"For one thing, the string of girlfriends." Rebecca rested her head against the high back of her seat. "None of them has lasted longer than six months. I counted."

"You did? I'm flattered," he said. "Now as far as your boyfriends were concerned, I think the longest running was three months, tops. Until Steve, that is."

"Some of them lasted three months? Who?" she demanded.

"I think his name was Boyce. The one who grew hydroponic tomatoes in his bathroom," Rick said. "And maybe Frankie—no, Freddie. I never met a guy who owned so many different ties. I think he broke up with you when he realized he might have to repeat one."

She hardly even remembered Boyce, and Freddie hadn't made a much greater impression. "I'm surprised you noticed them."

"I notice everything about you," Rick said.

He sounded almost serious. Rebecca didn't believe it, though. "Name three things you've noticed about me."

"You're allergic to peanuts."

"Everybody knows that!"

"Your hair is naturally red, even though the gossips say it's dyed. I know because you never have dark roots and the hue never changes,'' he said.

"What gossips?'' she demanded. "Who says I dye my hair?''

"Everybody.'' He kept his expression sober, but she knew he must be joking. It was typical of Rick to try to get her goat.

"That's two things. What else?''

"You'd look great in a red fur bikini,'' he said.

Rebecca was tempted to toss her glass of water at him, but she cringed at the prospect of making a scene. Besides, Rick wouldn't hesitate to toss his back at her.

The waitress brought their food. It smelled so good that Rebecca decided to stop seeking a retort and let Rick win this skirmish in their war of words.

A distinguished-looking couple in their forties entered the diner. The woman had light blond hair, while her husband was dark. "Who are they?'' she asked.

Rick turned to look. "That's Nora Gates Forrester, my old piano teacher. She owns the local department store and serves on the town council. Byron's a terrific photographer.''

"What an interesting combination they make," Rebecca said.

"In this town, all sorts of unlikely people seem to fall in love." Rick frowned, as if puzzled by what he'd just said.

The Forresters paused to greet him, and seemed pleased to be introduced to Rebecca. She hoped they didn't think she was Rick's latest girlfriend.

After the pair moved on, she said, "I wondered where you learned to play so well." At parties, Rick had been known to toss off anything from rock to ragtime if there was a piano handy.

"I used to hate practicing, until I realized that it impressed people to hear me play," he admitted. "Because of football, most girls saw me as nothing more than a muscle-bound hunk. Throw in a piano and, well, I was irresistible."

Rebecca laughed. "And so modest."

"My deep and touching humility developed later," Rick said. "That was after I nearly got thrown off the football team for cutting practice and smarting off to the coach. I was a real pain in the neck, let me tell you."

"There's no need," Rebecca said.

"You already figured it out for yourself, huh?"

"I wasn't going to stoop low enough to say so. But I'm sure you've improved, oh, by leaps and bounds."

"I play piano better than I used to, anyway. Because I appreciate music for its own sake now." Rick paused to down another bite of hamburger.

His musical ability, Rebecca mused, was something she'd taken for granted about Rick. Seeing him in his hometown, obviously well-liked by many people, made her realize that there were a lot of things she'd taken for granted. His good humor, for one thing, and his reliability.

Reliability? Was she really using that word in connection with a guy who showed up half an hour late for the ballet and sometimes called at the last minute to cancel pizza plans when he had to work late?

But he was always around when it counted. The time she'd come down with flu and needed someone to run to the pharmacy, he'd not only done it but returned the next day to see if she needed anything else. When her battery died, stranding her at a shopping center, he'd left home in the middle of the World Series to jump-start her car.

Rebecca felt knocked for a loop. Surely she couldn't be seeing Rick in an entirely new way, after all these years, and yet...

The man sitting across from her wasn't merely handsome. He was warm and kind and generous. And he was always there when she needed him.

Rebecca gave herself a mental shake. In her hurt and confusion over Steve's betrayal, she was seeking refuge with the one man she should never count on too much.

She was trying to fit Rick into the mold of the man she wanted, the man she'd naively thought she'd found in Steve. But Rick wasn't Mr. Responsible. He wasn't a family man, a Rock of Gibraltar, or even her boyfriend. And no amount of wishing would make it so.

"Well?" Rick said, and she realized he must have asked her a question.

"I'm sorry," Rebecca said. "I'm kind of distracted today."

"I invited you to tour Casa Travis," he said. "Don't tell me you're not curious about the playboy's lair. As icing on the cake, I promise to play whatever you request on the piano. If I have the sheet music.''

''This isn't a ploy to get me to pick dirty laundry off the floor, is it?'' she teased.

Rebecca no longer felt the uneasiness that had troubled her in the past when Rick invited her to pop down to Tyler to see his house. She'd always managed to find excuses not to come, but now she couldn't remember why.

''I won't even ask you to scrub out the shower, unless you really, really want to,'' he said with mock solemnity. ''The truth is, I've been meaning to build a fire and try out the handheld popcorn popper my brother gave me for Christmas, but it didn't seem right to do it alone.''

''You mean, pop corn right over the fire?'' Rebecca was intrigued. The only poppers she'd ever seen depended on electricity. ''Can you do that? I mean, of course you can do that. What does the popper look like?''

''You'll have to see for yourself. Coming?''

''You bet.'' She couldn't wait to see Rick's house.

SOMETHING STRANGE WAS going on, Rick admitted to himself as he drove the few blocks between the diner and his house. For one thing, Becky had let him get away with that crack about her looking good in a red fur bikini. It wasn't like her not to come up with a sharp reply.

Of course, he had no doubt that she *would* look terrific in a bikini. And even better out of one.

These musings reminded him of something else that was odd. Since last night, he couldn't stop thinking about Becky, physically and emotionally.

Not that he'd ever been unaware of her, not since the day she and a girlfriend moved into the spare room of the student apartment he'd shared with another guy. She was too vibrant to ignore. But it had become clear to Rick early on that there would be nothing easy or casual about a romance that involved the two of them.

They would burn hot for a while, then flame out, leaving only ashes. He preferred to keep Becky as a friend.

But since last night, he could barely control himself. Maybe it had something to do with seeing her in a bridal gown. That virginal white, with a hint of cleavage at the neckline, had been delectable.

He knew, of course, that she didn't sleep with guys, because she'd told him so. Maybe that's what had made her so vulnerable to Steve. The woman's suppressed sexuality was overwhelming her better judgment.

Rick had yielded to the temptation to sleep with the wrong woman at times, and later regretted the misunderstandings that resulted. For a guy, passion and lasting love didn't necessarily go hand in hand. Not for some women, either. But with Becky, it would be different.

He knew that, intellectually. Now he just had to convince his daydreams.

THE HOUSE SURPRISED HER. The wood-frame structure looked ordinary enough outside, but inside it had been decorated with exquisite taste.

The wooden floors were burnished to dark gold. The motif of the sprigged curtains was repeated in the decorative wallpaper strips, while traditional-style furniture blended smoothly with what appeared to be a few genuine antiques. As for the framed landscape photographs, with their dramatic lighting and composition, they were far from ordinary.

In his college days, Rick's idea of decorating

had been to tack ragged photos of football players to the walls. She couldn't believe he had created this striking effect.

"Who picked all this?" Rebecca asked. "Don't tell me you did it yourself."

"Mostly, but I also consulted with our town celebrity. Ever hear of Susannah Atkins Santori?" he asked.

The name rang a bell. "Doesn't she write books about lifestyles?"

"That's her," Rick said. "I ran into her at the library while I was checking out books on decorating. She gave me a few tips. Even came over here once and made some suggestions. But mostly, this place reflects my choices."

"I'm surprised." She wandered through a doorway, and found herself in the kitchen. Larger than she would have expected, it featured butcher-block counters, tile floors and oak cabinets with beveled glass panes. "Gee, I'd forgotten that you cook."

Rick used to whip up omelettes and the occasional gourmet dish when they roomed together. But she hadn't seen him so much as pick up a pan in recent years.

"I haven't had much time, but I figure eventually I will," he said. "Besides, I plan to marry someday and have kids. Susannah says the kitchen is the heart of a home, and I agree."

A pang of envy gripped Rebecca. One of these days, Rick would share this delightful house with a wife. Who would he pick? she wondered. Maybe there was a hometown girl she didn't know about.

"Got anyone in mind?" she asked.

"For what?"

"Never mind." If he had a girlfriend, he would have told her.

"I promised to play for you, remember?" He escorted her back into the living room, where he lifted the wooden cover from the keyboard of his upright piano. "What's your request?"

"'The Moonlight Sonata,'" she blurted. Although she loved the haunting piece of music, she didn't really believe he could play it.

Rick opened the bench, flipped through some sheet music and took out a book entitled *Beloved Classics*. Placing it on a rack above the keyboard, he sat down to play.

Rebecca took a seat on a chair nearby. She tried not to stare at Rick, but she couldn't help it. With his long legs poised at the piano pedals and his classic profile riveted on the sheet music, he seemed timeless and traditional and infinitely masculine.

She felt certain that, once he married a woman and brought her here, he would never stray. A man who spent so much care creating a home would never treat it lightly.

His hands moved across the keys, and rippling waves of music lifted Rebecca into a starry night. She sensed vast distances and the cold wash of moonlight, but also the saving warmth of a cherished companion.

In the emotional upwelling of the music, she felt the true sensitivity of Rick's nature. This was indeed a different man than the one she'd thought she knew.

This must be the self he would share with a wife. A hollow place opened inside Rebecca at the realization that this part of Rick would belong to someone else.

He stopped playing. "You look on the verge of tears. Was it that bad?"

"You're terrific," she said. "I didn't realize the music would affect me that way."

"It's because of what you've gone through. Don't pretend that breaking off a wedding isn't wrenching,'' Rick said. "I'll tell you what. Why don't I build a fire and we can pop some corn, as promised?''

Although she wasn't hungry, Rebecca agreed. By the time flames leaped in the fireplace and kernels began bursting in a flat wire basket shaken on its long handle, the scent gave her an appetite, after all.

"This is great,'' she admitted as the two of them sat on the couch, sharing a large bowl of salted popcorn. "The smoke gives it a special flavor.''

"Being together gives it a special flavor,'' he said.

Startled, Rebecca met his moody gaze. Surely he couldn't mean that in any romantic sense. "You mean sharing it with a friend?''

"Not exactly.'' Rick spoke tightly. "Surely you've noticed... Haven't you felt anything different between us?''

She couldn't lie about it. "Yes. I figured it would pass.''

"Do you want it to?''

"What are the options?'' Rebecca said.

"Spoken like a businesswoman.'' He smiled.

"Well, we could avoid being alone with each other until it seems safe. That's number one."

"I don't care for that option." Retreat would be cowardly, she told herself. Besides, she needed her friend at a time like this.

"We could go into therapy and talk this thing to death," Rick drawled.

"Yeah, right." She waited impatiently to hear option number three.

"There's a riskier strategy, although it has a certain appeal." He folded his hands behind his head and stretched out his legs.

"Shoot," she said.

"The way I figure it, if we follow our instincts, sooner or later we'll dissolve into laughter," he said. "Or get cranky and start pinching each other. Then this tension will dissipate once and for all."

Rebecca admitted to herself that she would be disappointed if that happened, but he was right. Her desire to kiss Rick and let him touch her breasts again couldn't possibly lead much further. Not between the two of them.

"I've never gone in for heavy petting," she warned him. "I'm not sure this is a good idea."

"I'm out of options," he said. "What would you suggest?"

"Give me a minute." Restlessly, Rebecca carried the empty popcorn bowl into the kitchen and washed her hands. She heard Rick moving around, running the water in the bathroom sink, and knew he was rinsing his hands, too.

Would it be so terrible to indulge in a few more kisses? Any day now, Rick might meet the woman he would decide to marry, and then Rebecca would have no more opportunities.

Besides, it was a way to armor herself against the next man she mistook for Mr. Right. If she'd realized how strongly attracted she felt to Rick, she would have known that she couldn't spend her life married to Steve, or anyone who failed to arouse the same level of desire.

It was friendship that swayed her, in the end. It would be best to work this nonsense out of their systems so they could get back to being pals.

When she returned to the living room, Rick was again sitting on the couch. With the curtains drawn against the blustery day, the fire bathed him in an intimate glow.

"Okay," she said. "How do we do this?"

He grinned. "I never thought about it before. The moves are supposed to come naturally."

Rebecca relaxed. "Maybe we've already reached the part where we dissolve into laughter."

"I'll tell you what," he said. "Come sit on my lap and we'll talk about it. Take your shoes off first." He'd already followed his own advice, she saw.

Self-consciously, Rebecca removed her walking shoes and tucked her thick hair behind her ears. She wished she'd thought to check her makeup, then remembered that it was likely to get smeared anyway.

"Here goes nothing," she said, and sat on Rick's lap.

Instantly, she became aware of him in all sorts of ways. Of his muscular chest, and the alluring scent of his aftershave lotion. Of the way that, beneath her sensitive bottom, a part of him was springing to life.

"Mistake," she said.

"You haven't even kissed me yet."

That would be safe enough, she decided. Kissing was allowable, even on her puritanical checklist. "Okay." Resting one forearm on his shoulder, she tilted her face toward his.

Rick cupped her chin with one hand and stroked his thumb along her jawline. His lips grazed hers. So gentle. So safe.

Rebecca nestled against him. Rick ran his hands through her hair, kissed her lightly again, and reclined her backwards a few degrees in the crook of one arm.

Her breasts tightened in response. Rebecca considered stopping, but last night they'd gone this far, and no harm done.

Rick lowered one shoulder of her V-necked sweater and slipped down her bra. His lips found the nub of her breast and coaxed it to an almost painful peak. Excitement radiated through her.

He eased down more of her clothing, and explored the other breast. Rebecca's back arched as she urged him on.

Any minute now, they would both decide this was ridiculous. Any minute now, they would stop. But not yet. It felt too luxuriously good.

"Let's get these clothes out of the way," Rick said, and lifted off her sweater and bra. He tossed his plaid shirt onto the floor beside them. "Better."

His hands cupped her breasts as Rebecca knelt facing him, her pants-clad legs straddling his thighs. He pulled her closer, so their chests pressed together. It was thrilling to explore his bare skin with her own.

They kissed again, long and slow. Both of them were breathing hard by the time he lifted his head.

"Having second thoughts?" Rick asked.

She ought to, Rebecca reflected vaguely. But this felt so natural and right. "Maybe...just a little longer."

"I want to see what you look like." In his voice rasped a hoarse note that she'd never heard before.

"What do you mean?"

"I'll show you." He lifted her and deftly undid her slacks, stroking them down her thighs and adjusting her position so he could pull them clear. "Now let me look at you."

Rebecca should have felt self-conscious, but with such obvious admiration shining on Rick's face, how could she? Thank goodness she'd worn lacy underthings, which was all she'd brought on her honeymoon.

Honeymoon. The word reminded her that it

should be her husband studying her bare waist-line and navel and hips. But Rick was the closest thing to a husband. He was her friend.

He sat her on the couch beside him and slowly ran his palms along the insides of her thighs. Delicious, demanding heat rose inside Rebecca.

She'd been a little afraid of what she might experience when she made love with a man. But this felt enticingly suspenseful. Not that she was going to make love with Rick but at least now she knew there was nothing to be frightened of, and a tremendous amount to look forward to.

"You have a great body," she admitted, unable to resist caressing the muscular bulges and smooth stomach. "And your arms are so powerful. Do you still do push-ups every day?"

"Fifty, if my elbow isn't too sore," he said. "Let me demonstrate."

"You're going to do push-ups now?"

"I'll show you." His hands caught her shoulders and lowered her to the couch. From a kneeling position between her legs, he braced his hands on either side of her chest and performed a push-up right on top of her.

Rebecca started to laugh, and then discovered she didn't want to. Not with Rick's chest tight against her breasts and his hardness pressing into her core. She wanted him to do that again, and a lot more.

Instead, he lifted himself away and ran the heels of his hands along her thighs, right to her center. He was touching her in a place she'd never been touched before, stirring her in a new way, making her want fulfillment more than she'd ever imagined she could want anything.

"Rick," she whispered, and somehow managed to unsnap his jeans. With his help, she pushed them down. Vaguely, she realized he'd removed her underpants and his own clothing, and that he was unrolling something onto his hardness.

Rebecca couldn't think. She didn't want to think. She ached so fiercely that she could hardly bear the delay.

"Are you sure you want to do this?" Rick asked breathlessly.

"Yes," she whispered. "Oh, yes."

He eased her legs apart, and she felt his largeness slowly penetrate her. In the recesses of Rebecca's brain, a warning signal sounded. This was going to hurt.

But she wanted this kind of hurt. Wanted it

so much that she caught his hips and anchored herself against him, demanding more.

Unable to restrain himself, he thrust into her. There was a sharp pang, and then the relief of being filled completely by him.

"Are you okay?" Rick asked.

"More than okay," Rebecca said. "It's wonderful."

"For me, too." He moved in and out, inflaming her already heightened senses. Curving down, he nibbled her breasts, then kissed her again. His tongue mirrored what his body was doing, claiming her, then withdrawing.

"Is it always like this?" she asked in amazement.

"No." His expression softened until she could have sworn his eyes glowed. "It feels so good I'm not sure I can take as long as I'd like."

"It's perfect already."

"You're not even halfway there," he said.

She couldn't imagine what "there" might be. And then he showed her.

The thrusting grew longer and fiercer. It was exhilarating the way her body responded of its own accord, arching, urging, matching him in intensity.

How had she lived this long without knowing she was capable of such pleasure? And that Rick was the man who could arouse her to it?

She was joyously aware of sharing everything with him. Their connection surpassed anything she'd dreamed of, and yet she was still herself. Not overwhelmed but free.

The sensations intensified. She was out of control, and she loved it. Loved being anchored to Rick, and loved the carnival colors exploding around her.

She couldn't stop to think about the implications. For once in her twenty-seven years, Rebecca stopped calculating and simply let life claim her.

CHAPTER FIVE

RICK HADN'T MEANT for them to go this far, even though he'd taken the precaution of bringing some protection from the bathroom. He'd tried to make sure, at every step, that Becky was completely comfortable with what they were doing.

Then he'd lost all caution in the splendor of lovemaking and of his transcendent climax. It wasn't anything physical that caused it, although in his eyes Becky was unquestionably beautiful. It was that, for the first time, he shared true intimacy of spirit and body.

Afterwards, he removed the protection, tucked it into a towel on the floor and lay beside her, holding her tightly against him on the narrow couch. It hadn't been the most elegant of places to make love, but neither of them seemed to mind.

"I hope it was as good for you as it was for me," he said.

"Hmm?" Becky murmured dreamily. Her russet hair enveloped them both, and, in the afterglow, her skin had a rare creaminess.

Usually after sex Rick felt sleepy or hungry or both. This time, he just wanted to lie here holding Becky, to merge her happiness with his own.

"You don't mind?" he said.

"Mind what?" She shifted a little.

"That we—that I—you know. Your first time."

"Neither of us planned it." Becky's brain had started working again. He could tell when she wriggled from his arms and sat up. "It seemed like a reasonable idea to get this out of our systems. Who would have thought…"

She stopped, frowning. Uneasily, Rick followed her gaze to the towel.

"Where did that come from?" she asked.

He wished he'd hidden the darned thing. "I thought it was a wise precaution to bring some protection. So you wouldn't have to worry about getting pregnant, if—"

"If?" she repeated. He didn't like the tension in her voice.

"Let's not get hung up on details," Rick said. "Becky, what happened is special."

"You planned this." Storm clouds gathered in her eyes. "That whole business about dissolving into laughter, you didn't believe that, did you?"

"I thought it was possible we might start chuckling. Or that we might not." Rick finger-combed his hair from his forehead. "I didn't know how far you'd go. Becky, it's been driving me crazy, thinking about holding you."

"So you decided to get it out of *your* system!" Her forehead puckered, a sure sign of anger. "You said you didn't know how far I'd go. Obviously, you knew how far you would go, or wanted to go. You manipulated me, Rick."

Had he? "Not intentionally," he said with a sinking feeling.

"And I thought I could trust you!" Her voice trembled as she grabbed her clothes off the floor. "You're just like Steve!"

Indignantly, Rick reached for his own clothes. "I'm sorry you see it that way, but I didn't betray you."

"Then why do I feel betrayed?"

"Because you recently suffered a shock and

it's made you paranoid,'' he said. ''Becky, I would never do anything to hurt you.''

''I'm sure Steve would have gotten around to that line if I'd given him enough time!'' To his dismay, Rick saw tears glistening in her eyes.

''Come here, sweetheart.'' He sat back on the couch. ''We need to hold each other and talk about this.''

''Sweetheart?'' She continued yanking on her clothes. ''Is that what you call all your girl-friends?''

''You're not... I mean...'' He didn't know what he meant. Was Becky his girlfriend now? He didn't think of her the same way as other women he'd dated.

''You're right, I'm not your girlfriend.'' She got her sweater on backwards and, to her obvious fury, had to pull it up and turn it around. ''Take me home, Rick.''

''All the way to Madison?'' he asked.

''You know what I mean!''

How had things gone so wrong? he wondered miserably. ''Can I put my clothes on first?''

''Whatever.'' She stalked toward the bath-room.

Rick buried his face in his hands. He should

have listened to his better judgment and kept a distance between him and Becky.

Why couldn't she accept that what had happened between them was on a different plane than any other experience? They needed to proceed from here, without torturing themselves about motives or might-have-beens.

But maybe that wasn't possible. If he suggested it, no doubt she would accuse him of being self-serving. Life had suddenly become much too complicated, and Rick didn't know how to untangle the mess.

When Becky returned, her face had been washed and her hair combed. And her expression had hardened into an accusation.

"You *did* send that awful fur bikini and jock strap, didn't you?" she asked in a low voice.

"What?" Such a possibility had been the furthest thing from Rick's mind. "No! Give me some credit, Becky. Besides, you said the guy ordered the stuff on Friday. As far as I knew on Friday, you were going to be honeymooning with Steve."

She mulled his answer. "All right. Unless I can figure out some way you could have known about Steve and Esther, you're in the clear about that one.''

"Are you going to accuse me of anything else?'' he asked. "Running up the national debt? Causing that heavy snowfall last month when you wanted to go shopping?''

"If the shoe fits, wear it,'' she said, and marched out of the house.

Rick didn't like to leave matters this way, but right now Becky was beyond reason. It was his own fault, for pushing her too far, too fast. She hadn't been ready to make love with a man so soon after losing her fiancé. He should have known that.

Resigned to at least a temporary coolness between them, he drove her to the Breakfast Inn Bed. The trouble was, he admitted silently as she jumped from the car and ran inside without waiting for him to open her door, that he didn't know what he wanted to happen next. He'd never been in this situation before.

He didn't just want Becky to be his girlfriend. He wanted her with him all the time, even if it meant a lot of fighting along the way.

His house was never going to be the same without her. He would always picture her the way she'd looked today, rumpled and relaxed, bubbling with joy. She belonged in his house, and she belonged with him.

The truth hit Rick halfway down Rose Street. He was in love with Becky.

It was scary. He hadn't felt at such an utter loss since the doctors told him his football career was at a premature end. Maybe not even then.

He'd found another career. He would never find another Becky.

Instinctively, Rick turned right on Gunther Street, then halted in front of the Kelsey Boarding House. He'd turned to his old football coach, Pam Kelsey, for advice after his injury, and she was the best person he could think of to consult now.

Set among middle-class frame homes, the spacious old house had a large porch and freshly painted trim. Johnny and Anna Kelsey had run it for years, and when their son Patrick, the high school basketball coach, married Pam, the pair had moved in here.

Pam had told Rick on his last visit that she'd once dreamed of having a home of her own. With occasional flare-ups of multiple sclerosis, however, and a young son to care for, she'd gladly accepted the hospitality of her in-laws in order to have them close by.

Rick knocked on the door. It was opened a moment later by a tall, willowy woman whom he recognized as a new waitress at Marge's Diner. Caroline was her name, he recalled. "Hi. Is Pam here? I'm Rick Travis."

"I'll tell her." With a friendly nod, she ushered him inside.

A minute later, Pam hurried to greet him with welcome shining in her brown eyes. Even in her early thirties, she still had the leanness of the Olympic runner she'd once been. "It's good to see you. Let's go in the den, where it's private."

She must have guessed that he wouldn't have arrived unannounced on a Sunday afternoon unless something were amiss. Rick wasn't sure whether he enjoyed being such an open book. "How are you?" With Pam, it wasn't an idle question, since there was always the danger that her illness might worsen.

"I have to be careful of my health, but I'm doing really well." There was a slight stiffness in her movements, but that might be due to football practice rather than to her chronic illness.

"The team had another winning season, so I'm in everyone's good graces."

"You don't need to tell me! I go to every game I can manage." He could hear conversation drifting from the living room, where the renters often gathered, and a creaking board overhead indicated someone was upstairs as well. "How's the family?"

Pam grinned. "Great. Jeremy's such a delight. I can't believe he'll be starting kindergarten next year."

"Where is the little tyke?" Rick enjoyed being around children.

"Patrick took him to a birthday party this afternoon. I guess he stayed there to help. He loves this kid stuff, and it gives me a little time by myself."

"Am I intruding?" Maybe she was supposed to be resting now, Rick thought guiltily.

"Socializing on an adult level counts as time by myself." Pam guided him into the overstuffed den. "Can I get you some coffee?"

"No, thanks. I'm still full from lunch at Marge's." And popcorn, he recalled.

"I heard you had a young lady with you," she prompted.

Rick released a long breath. "News sure travels fast in Tyler."

"Isn't it delightful?" Pam made no secret of her love for her adopted hometown. "Now tell me what's on your mind."

Even with an old friend like Pam, loyalty to Becky kept Rick from going into detail. All he said was, "She's someone I like a lot but I've offended her. I guess I didn't realize how much she meant to me until too late."

"You had a fight?" Pam guessed.

"I wish we could fight," he said. "I thought we fought all the time, but in fact what we did was friendly bickering. This time, she kind of froze me out."

"I take it there's more here than you care to disclose." The coach rocked back in her recliner, propping up her legs.

"You'd think, at my age, that I'd have all the right moves down pat," Rick said. "But I'm playing on unfamiliar territory here. This is one game I can't afford to lose."

"Have you told the lady how you feel?" Pam asked.

"She'd laugh at me." On second thought, laughter wouldn't be a bad response. "Worse, she'd get angry. She'd think I was making fun of her."

"You may have to be patient," Pam said. "Work your way back into her good graces."

"It won't be easy," Rick said. "She had a disastrous experience with another guy and it's made her doubly suspicious of me and my motives."

"Tomorrow's Valentine's Day," she pointed out. "It's a good time to make a fresh start."

Rick's spirits rose. Normally, Becky would distrust him even more if he showed up bearing gifts, but on Valentine's Day, it might not seem so out of character. "That's an idea."

"One tiff doesn't mean all is lost," Pam added. "Patrick and I had our ups and downs before we got together."

"Yeah, but that was because he wasn't so sure about having a female football coach," Rick reminded her.

"Neither were you."

"I gave you a rough time, didn't I?" he said.

"Not as rough as I gave you."

"I needed it." That year had marked a turning point in Rick's maturity. Without having learned humility and a sense of his own obligations after nearly getting kicked off the team, he'd have had a much harder time dealing with the end of his football career years later.

"Love takes work, as much as any sport," Pam said. "If you care about this woman, you'll stick around until she sees that you're sincere."

"I'm willing to do that," Rick said. "I just hope she won't hold a grudge."

A short time later, he took his leave, not wanting to use up all of Pam's rest time. He felt somewhat better, but couldn't quite share the coach's confidence about his future.

He knew from experience how stubborn Becky could be. She might forgive him, or she might stick him in the same mental category as Steve and keep him there.

Rick's mind whirred with plans as he returned to his car. The ad agency where he worked allowed its employees to take one floating holiday per year, an option he'd never used. Tomorrow he would take the day off and hit the stores as soon as they opened.

One romance, coming up. If he had anything to say about it.

REBECCA COULDN'T believe she'd managed to lose two men in one weekend. All night, as she tossed and turned in bed, images played through her mind.

Hardly any of them concerned Steve. Instead, she kept seeing Rick greeting his friends at Marge's Diner and introducing them to Rebecca. Rick playing "The Moonlight Sonata," which in her dream sounded strangely like "Love Me Tender." Rick popping corn over the fire in his house.

Rebecca's whole body echoed with his absence. Once, she awoke from the safety of his arms to find herself alone, and even the quilt couldn't stop her shivering.

She couldn't be friends with him anymore, not after what he'd done. After what *they'd* done, she amended, willing to accept partial responsibility.

She'd been naive and impulsive. Those traits might be reprehensible in her well-ordered world, but they paled compared to his deviousness.

In the end, the man she'd believed was her best friend had treated her like any other woman that he wanted to take to bed. That knowledge hurt more than anything.

For Rebecca, making love with him had been an amazing experience. She wasn't sorry she'd done it. She hoped that Mr. Right, when she found him, would understand. In fact, since he wasn't likely to be a virgin himself, he had better understand or she would give him a swift boot out the door.

She used to picture Mr. Right as looking a little like Brad Pitt without the scraggly chin hair. Now the only image she could summon was of a tall, dark-haired, clean-shaven man with broad shoulders and sky-blue eyes.

This too would pass, she told herself. And tried her best to believe it.

AFTER BREAKFASTING in her room on Monday morning, Rebecca dressed in the outfit she'd brought for Valentine's Day. The silky red shell top and matching flare skirt were topped by a heart-covered white jacket with a high collar and puff-shouldered sleeves.

She wore it for herself, to celebrate having survived false love. Besides, Rick might come looking for her. She didn't want him to think she was down in the dumps about what had happened.

No, he would be at work by now, maybe even boasting to some of his male friends about his conquest. That wasn't his usual style, but at this point, she wouldn't put anything past him.

She debated whether to take a stroll around Tyler. It would be fun to explore the shops. On the other hand, what if she ran into someone she'd met yesterday who blithely assumed she was dating Rick?

A loud knock sent Rebecca's heart skittering around her chest cavity. Rick!

She smoothed her skirt and ran a quick brush through her hair, trying not to hurry. It might help, she thought as she observed herself in the mirror, if she wiped that relieved expression off her face. So what if he cared enough to skip work?

The knock came again. "Open up, Rebecca!" It was her mother's voice.

Her heart tumbled into free fall. Rick hadn't come. Worse, her mother might have brought the only other man in the world that Rebecca never wanted to see again.

She approached the door. "Is there anyone with you?"

"Yes!" her mother said. "Esther."

Rebecca didn't particularly want to see her former friend. On the other hand, Diane Salber deserved more respect than to be left standing in the hall.

When Rebecca opened the door, her two visitors gaped at her. Apparently they'd been expecting something other than a fully dressed, beautifully groomed woman. Thank goodness makeup hid the dark circles under her eyes.

"Hi, Mom," Rebecca said. "Isn't this a terrific bed and breakfast? I could get some hot chocolate and a muffin for you." Reluctantly, she added, "You, too, Esther."

"Thank you, but we've eaten." Diane came inside. She wore a pale pink suit that set off her dark hair, but Rebecca detected pallor in her mother's complexion.

"Are you okay?" she asked. "I know this weekend has been tough on you, but the worst is over." She hoped it was, anyway.

Diane's chin lifted. "Both of us owe you an apology."

"Not you! I'm the one who left you to deal with the wedding guests."

"Yes, I do." Her mother squared her shoulders. "I had a long talk with Esther last night and discovered you were right. She and Steve, well, did something they shouldn't have. I'm sorry for doubting you.''

"Oh, Mom!"

"I..." Esther cleared her throat. "I'm sorry, too, Becky. I said some mean things. Jealousy is an ugly trait, and I shouldn't give in to it.''

"And?'' Diane prompted.

Esther twirled a finger nervously through her wispy dark-blond hair. She'd worn a bright yellow shirtwaist dress that didn't suit her complexion. "And I'm sorry about your wedding. My parents were really mad when they found out what happened.''

"Esther's offered to pay part of the costs, and Steve is going to pay the rest,'' her mother said. "I think that's a positive step.''

A step toward what? Rebecca wondered. "Good,'' she said. "Did you really drive to Tyler just to tell me this?''

"Steve wants to talk to you.'' Diane held up one hand to forestall her protest. "He's absolutely miserable.''

"I'll agree with that,'' Rebecca couldn't resist saying.

"You might give him a chance!'' Esther

flared. "He's so embarrassed. Apparently this whole mess might hurt his business."

"He's the one who chose to invite some of his best clients and then gave me cause to cancel the wedding," Rebecca said. "I hardly think he's the injured party here."

"He regrets what he did," her mother said.

"No, he—" Esther halted. "I mean, yes, he does."

A nasty suspicion sprang up. In retrospect, one of the reasons Steve might have singled Rebecca out in the first place was that she worked for an accounting firm that was one of his clients, and was known and respected by officers of several other companies whose accounts she handled.

Now Steve was apparently concerned that his ruined wedding had made a bad impression on his contacts. He might have persuaded Esther that he and Rebecca needed to marry, but that he would keep her as his "true love." Was he capable of such duplicity? And was the bridesmaid capable of such gullibility?

"Exactly what is going on between you and Steve?" she asked.

"N-nothing."

"Nothing at all?" Rebecca pressed. "He wants to marry me because he adores me and can't stand to live without me, is that what he told you?"

"Kind of," Esther muttered.

"So he never cared about you." She pressed on, trying for maximum provocation to force out the truth. "It was like he said, just a case of prewedding jitters."

Esther's eyes flashed. "No, it wasn't! We love each other."

"Esther!" Diane exclaimed. "We discussed this."

"I said I would apologize because—well, my parents would kill me if I didn't," Esther said. "And Steve asked me to help out. But I'm the one he loves!"

The coldness of Diane's gaze silenced her. "I left Steve a note this morning about where we were going. No doubt he'll arrive soon himself and we can straighten this out."

Esther's indignation withered. "He might say—I mean, Rebecca's important to his career. That doesn't mean…"

Someone rapped at the door with a fast, self-conscious rhythm.

"Shall I let him in?" Rebecca asked Esther. "Maybe you two would like to get your stories straight first."

"That won't be necessary," said Diane, and went to the door.

CHAPTER SIX

RICK'S ARMS ACHED from the weight of the shopping bag and the spray of red roses. He'd also worn a business suit as a sign of respect. It was going a bit overboard, he supposed, but Becky deserved it.

He was preparing his best laid-back smile when the door opened and he found himself face to face with Diane Salber, whose own smile mutated rapidly into an expression of dismay. "What are you doing here?" she demanded.

"The ad agency doesn't pay enough, so I took a second job delivering for the local department store," he deadpanned.

"Rick?" Becky peered around her mother. "We thought you were Steve."

So that low-life was expected to show his face here today. Rick couldn't help but be grateful. Why else would there be a reluctant plea for support in Becky's green eyes?

The errant bridegroom had already given Rick one big break by driving her to call off their wedding. Apparently he was providing a second one, forcing her to rely on her pal's support just when he needed to get on her good side.

"I'll stick around, by all means." Diane remained planted, blocking him, but Rick edged forward until his roses were practically in her face. No doubt realizing she was on the verge of making a scene, she yielded.

Becky regarded the shopping bag and the flowers in confusion. "Where did those come from?"

"He's a delivery boy," snapped Esther, whom Rick hadn't noticed before. "Didn't you hear him?"

"That was a joke." He angled the flowers toward Becky until she took them. "From me to you. There's more." From within the bag, he handed her a box of candied fruits, which he knew she loved, even though he himself would have preferred chocolates. "Happy Valentine's Day."

He left the other gifts out of sight in the depths of the bag. They were too personal to share in front of others.

Emotions fleeted across Becky's face too rapidly for him to read them. "Thank you," she said, and set the candy on a table.

"Sweetheart gifts, huh?" Esther regarded him with malevolent triumph. "I knew it!"

Diane fetched a vase from the mantelpiece and set aside the silk flowers it contained. "I'll get some water." She snatched the roses and headed for the bathroom.

"You can't deny the obvious, Becky," Esther said. "You never loved Steve the way I do. It's Rick you wanted all along, isn't it?"

"Don't jump to conclusions." It was hardly a declaration of undying love, but it was a lot milder than other things Becky could have said about him, Rick decided. And that she probably would have said if she hadn't had visitors.

"You don't want Steve back," Esther went on. "So why waste his time coming here?"

"As you'll recall, I'm not the one who invited him." The words bristled with irritation.

Diane returned and set the roses in a corner. "You'll talk to him, though. He's a good, steady man, Rebecca."

"I haven't found him either good or steady." Becky was keeping a tight grip on her temper,

Rick could see, but with an obvious effort. "And I'm only going to listen to him out of respect for you, Mom."

"I hate this!" Esther burst out. "I hate the fact that he's going to kowtow to her when he doesn't even love her! I hate the fact that he considers her a suitable wife to parade in front of his clients even though he loves me. It's love that counts, not other people's opinions!"

"Excuse me," Rick said. "Why are you debating this with Becky? Isn't this something you should take up with good buddy Steve?"

Diane frowned at him. "I don't see how this concerns you."

"Of course it concerns him!" cried Esther. "Look at the two of them. They're obviously dressed for a date."

"We didn't have a date," he said. "As far as Becky knew, I would be at work now."

"So you decided to surprise her?" Esther's words dripped with sarcasm. "How thoughtful."

"It really doesn't matter why he's here," Diane said. "Her groom is about to arrive, and I don't want anything or anyone to interfere. That includes you, Rick."

"I'm not going," he said.

"Neither am I," said Esther.

"Rebecca?" asked her mother. "Would you please give me some support here?"

Wearily, Becky regarded her stubborn guests. "Okay. *All* of you can leave. I'm tired of having other people try to make up my mind for me. Even you, Mom, although I know you mean well."

Before she could throw them out, however, Molly Spencer appeared in the open doorway with a package. "This just came." She glanced at the crowd of people. "Sorry for disturbing you."

"Not at all. Thanks for bringing it." Becky's eyes narrowed as she took the package, which bore the same wrappings as the previous two gifts from the novelty shop.

"Where did that come from?" Diane asked.

"If it's like the other stuff I've received, it was ordered Friday in Lake Geneva," Becky said. Discreetly, Molly withdrew.

"What other stuff?" asked Esther.

"Tacky stuff," Becky said, and ripped off the wrappings. From the gift box, she pulled a pair of pink boxer shorts. An oversize red heart enclosed the fly opening.

"Is this someone's idea of a joke?" Diane asked.

Rick plucked a card from the box and read aloud, "Right after my honeymoon, I'll be coming over to console you. Who needs that loser of a husband when you can have me? Love from your new admirer, Steve."

He turned the card over, wondering if this puzzling message came with an explanation. There was no other notation, however.

"He actually signed this one? He must have decided it was time to make his move, but on whom?" Becky asked. Pressing close to Rick, she reread the note over his shoulder. "This couldn't have been intended for me, or for Esther, either. She doesn't have a husband."

They were so close that Rick could smell her flowery shampoo. With an effort, he quelled his instinct to loop one arm around Becky's waist. It might embarrass her. Also, he wasn't eager to get slapped.

"This is a trick you're playing to get back at me, right?" the bridesmaid demanded. "You're trying to make it look like Steve was chasing somebody else at the same time he was seducing me. Well, I don't believe it!''

"Maybe you ought to show us the stuff that arrived earlier.'' A steely reserve had replaced Diane's earlier determination.

From the closet, Becky pulled the red fake-fur bikini and jock strap. "This is what came, with notes of the 'I want your body' variety. They weren't signed, but it would be reasonable to assume they're also from Steve.''

"We called the gift shop,'' Rick added. "They said a man ordered them Friday in a big hurry. We're assuming he got the addresses switched.''

Diane grimaced. "Steve must have some good explanation, but I can't imagine what it is.''

"You could search five states and not find anything as ugly as these,'' Rick couldn't resist adding.

"He was probably kidding around,'' Esther said defiantly. "Obviously, he meant them for you, Becky. It's a joke.''

"A joke about seducing someone else after our honeymoon?'' she asked.

"Excuse me.'' In the hallway, Molly hurried

into view. She was a little out of breath from taking the stairs fast. ''There's a man here to see Rebecca. I asked him to wait. It occurred to me you might like a little advance notice.''

''Oh, yes!'' Becky said.

''Please give us about five minutes, then send him up,'' Diane said. Molly nodded and left. ''I think it's best if he and Rebecca have a chance to talk by themselves.''

''I think it's best if I never see him again. But I suppose I have to.'' Becky reached into a drawer and took out a small object. Rick couldn't see what it was and decided not to be nosy.

''I'll stick around if you want me to,'' he offered.

''Sure,'' she said. ''You're my man of honor, after all.''

Diane grabbed Esther's wrist. ''Well, Steve doesn't need to see us. We're going in the bathroom. Now!'' The bridesmaid glowered, but obeyed.

''How're you holding up?'' Rick asked when the other two had retreated.

''Shakily,'' Becky admitted. ''I'm sure I'll

run into him sooner or later, so we might as well have it out now.''

''Let's hide the evidence.'' Rick stuffed the gag gifts into his shopping bag, out of sight but close at hand. ''Let me know if you want me to deck him.''

''Feeling protective?'' she asked.

''Very,'' he said.

''Good, because for some reason, I'm feeling in need of protection.'' The warmth in her gaze gave him a ray of hope. Then it vanished.

''I don't really need protection. I can take care of myself,'' Becky said. ''Anyway, after what happened, we can't go back to being the way we were.''

''I know.''

Did he just imagine the alarm in her widened eyes and parted lips? All he'd done was to agree with her. Rick wondered how she'd interpreted, or misinterpreted, his remark.

He never got a chance to find out, because here came Steve, whistling down the hall.

There was nothing in the man's chipper demeanor to indicate he'd lost sleep or even a moment's peace over ruining his wedding. His slightly pudgy face looked well-rested, his brown eyes were clear, and he was smiling.

"You look great, Rebecca!" he said. "Your mom must have told you I was coming."

"I didn't wear this for you," she replied frostily.

He gave her an unwrapped box of candy. It was, Rick saw, peanut clusters. "Happy Valentine's Day."

"I'm allergic to peanuts, but thanks anyway." She handed the box to Rick. "He'll enjoy them."

Steve spared his rival an annoyed glance. "I'm sure my wife appreciates your sticking around as maid of honor—oh, I'm sorry, that's man of honor, isn't it?—but it's time for you to make yourself scarce."

"I'd prefer that he stay," Becky said. "First of all, I'm not your wife. And second, anything you want to tell me can be said in front of him."

"I'm the soul of discretion," Rick added with mock sincerity.

Steve couldn't hide his irritation, but he managed to swallow it. "All right. I want to apologize for that business with Esther. You know how it is."

"I do?"

"She made it clear she'd do anything to get me in bed, to spite you." He didn't seem to notice the choking sound coming from the bathroom. "I admit, I was weak. If you hadn't kept me at arm's length for so long, Becky, I'd have had more resistance."

"So this is my fault, because I didn't jump into your bed?"

"I didn't say that."

"In any case, you're not in love with Esther?" she asked.

"In love?" he sneered. "Honey, I can't even think about anyone but my beautiful Rebecca. When I was with Esther, I closed my eyes and pretended it was you."

The knob on the bathroom door rattled, as if someone were struggling to open it and being restrained. "Air pressure," Becky said when Steve glanced in that direction. "It's an old house, but cozy."

"Yeah, isn't the bed and breakfast concept too cutesy-pie for words?" he snorted. "I can't imagine who recommended this place."

"I did," Rick said.

"Oh, yeah, now I remember."

The guy was asking for a fight, but he had to know Rick was too civilized to give him one. Not much too civilized, though.

"So do we understand each other?" Steve asked Becky.

"I think I understand you loud and clear." She fiddled with the small object in her palm. Rick still couldn't see what it was.

"There's one thing I want to know," he told Steve.

"Sure. Then go someplace where you might actually be welcome," muttered the would-be groom.

"Who were these for?" Setting the candy aside, Rick pulled the red fake-fur items and the boxer shorts from the shopping bag.

Steve stared at them in shock. "What are they doing here? Those were for Connie." He halted, his arrogance vanishing as he realized what he'd admitted.

"Connie Graf? The banquet manager?" Becky looked almost as taken aback as Steve.

The tall, striking blonde was, Rick recalled, undergoing a marital separation. That explained the reference to a husband. But he had a hard time believing the nerve of a man who would sleep with one woman, plan to walk down the aisle with another and, at the same time, try to orchestrate the seduction of a third.

It took a monstrous ego and a ruthless willingness to exploit other people's vulnerabilities. The man was even more of a snake than Rick had realized.

The bathroom door flew open. "You were after Connie?" Diane flew out with Esther at her heels. "You planned to honeymoon with my daughter and then jump right into another woman's bed?"

Before he could reply, Esther added, "You were the one who said you loved me! I did *not* throw myself at you!"

Faced with both women at once, Steve struggled for words. The first one he addressed was Esther. "You must have misunderstood. I never said you chased me."

"Yes, you did!"

"No, I said...I mean..." For once, he couldn't come up with an excuse fast enough.

"You ordered those gifts for Connie on Friday," Diane said. "When exactly did he declare himself to you, Esther?"

"On Saturday." Her voice quavered. "He

gave me that hangdog look and whined about how he needed someone to show him what real love was like. I can't believe I fell for a complete lie!''

''You might have expected it from a guy who would cheat on his bride,'' Becky said. ''But I'm sorry he hurt you. I'm sorry either of us ever met this loser.''

''Your pride didn't stop you from accepting the diamond necklace I sent. It must have arrived by now, but you haven't even mentioned it, so I presume you intend to keep it.'' Steve drew himself up in a show of injured righteousness.

''What diamond necklace?'' Becky said.

''Don't play innocent with me!''

Her bewildered expression was, in Rick's estimation, completely unfeigned. ''You must have given the jewelry store the wrong address, too.''

''No, I'm sure I didn't...'' Steve paused as his almost-mother-in-law broke into a smile. ''What?''

''Oh, *that's* where it came from!'' Diane crowed. ''Connie was radiant this morning. She showed me a beautiful diamond necklace and said her husband sent it to her with the most loving note.''

''That was my Valentine's Day gift to Becky!'' Steve said.

''Well, it looks great on Connie,'' Diane told him. ''Joe showed up right before Esther and I left. He had the good sense not to admit the necklace wasn't from him. I think he believes the hotel staff sent it to help patch things up.''

''I want it back,'' Steve said. ''That thing cost me a fortune. I'll have to make payments for a year.''

''Joe Graf wouldn't be too happy to find out you were trying to seduce his wife,'' Diane said. ''You know, he used to be a professional boxer, and he has a notoriously short fuse.''

Steve's jaw worked as he stood there, fists clenched, absorbing the wreckage he had made of his love life. And, apparently, his finances.

''This isn't fair,'' he said.

Diane shrugged. ''I'd say it was more than fair.''

''Obviously, I can't also afford to pay for the wedding Rebecca decided to cancel.''

''I have that note you signed this morning, promising to reimburse half the wedding expenses," said Becky's mother. "If you don't pay, I'm not only suing you for damages but for emotional distress and anything else I can think of."

"Here." Becky handed him the object she'd been holding. It was her engagement ring. "You can sell this. I certainly don't want it."

Steve pocketed it. "All right, I'll pay, Mrs. Salber, if you insist," he growled. "But I plan to double-check every penny of those expenses! Come on, Esther, let's blow this joint."

"Me?" asked the bridesmaid. "You expect me to go with you, after what's happened?"

"Those things I told you when we were together, they were true." Steve waved one hand vaguely, as if he didn't remember the details. "You're my sweetheart, right?" Apparently he was determined to save face by walking out of here with a woman, no matter how little he cared about her.

Tears slipped down the woman's cheeks. Despite what she'd done to Becky, Rick felt sorry for her.

"I'm not going anywhere with you," Esther said. "Because of you and my own petty jealousy, I've damaged the best friendship I ever had. I'm starting over in every way, and that includes having nothing to do with a jerk like you.''

''You expect me to leave here empty-handed?'' Steve demanded. The man's ego was positively dazzling, Rick thought.

''Empty-handed? Certainly not,'' Diane said with a gleam in her eye.

''We wouldn't dream of it,'' said Becky.

Mother and daughter grabbed the red fur garments and threw them into Steve's face. Rick contemplated throwing the box of peanut clusters too, but he didn't want to waste them.

''Now get out!'' Esther yelled, and pitched the pink heart-inscribed boxer shorts onto his head.

Steve backed into the hall, nearly colliding with Quinn Spencer. The innkeeper raised an eyebrow as he observed the garment-bedecked ex-bridegroom.

''Need any help?'' he asked.

Furious, Steve snatched the underpants off his head and the furry bra from his throat. He marched off, seemingly unaware of the red fur jock strap dangling over one shoulder.

Quinn rescued the stray garments from the

floor and handed them to Rick before continuing on his way to the upper floor. Esther threw her arms around Becky. "I'm so sorry!" she said. "I was an idiot."

"It's okay," Becky said. "In the long run, you did me a favor."

Diane turned to Rick. "I apologize for giving you a hard time. I'm glad you were here today."

"So am I," he said.

"Come on, Esther." Diane took the younger woman's arm. "Let's go drown our sorrows in a big lunch, and then I need to go to work."

After brief farewells, they departed. Rick was alone with Becky, which was exactly where he wanted to be.

He wished he didn't feel so nervous, but this was the most important moment of his life. And if he weren't careful, he might blow it.

SEEING STEVE thoroughly vanquished and humiliated should have elevated Rebecca's spirits. Instead, she felt only sadness.

Rick had agreed that they couldn't go back to being friends. It was thoughtful of him to bring the roses and candy as a peace offering, but was this simply a polite way of making an exit from her life?

Her heart had lifted when she saw him standing at the door. Among the confusion, she'd seen him as a rock she could hold on to, until he told her they couldn't be friends anymore.

Now, too late, she recognized that he'd been her rock for a long time. When had she started depending on Rick? Rebecca wondered. Months ago, or years? She couldn't even put a starting date to it.

Restlessly, she perched on the edge of the couch. "I can't believe Steve mixed up the addresses. Maybe it was a Freudian slip." She knew she was babbling to fill the silence, but she couldn't stop. "At some level, he must have felt guilty."

"Tell me what you saw in him." Rick took a seat beside her. "What made you think he was the man you wanted to spend your life with?" He seemed to care very much about her answer.

Rebecca searched her memory. "I thought he was someone I could rely on. Not like my father, who was always looking for a good time."

"The way you thought I was?" he prodded.

Her eyes stung with tears. "Yes."

Rick scanned her with an emotion that might almost be taken for tenderness. "I dated a lot of people, didn't I? But you were the woman I always came back to."

"Your best buddy." Rebecca's voice caught. "But I knew you'd never let anyone take away your freedom. With Steve, I thought I could control him. I don't mean like a robot, but that he would share the future I wanted, being married, having children, doing the things that were important to me."

Rick propped his elbows on his knees as he considered her words. "You thought he was compatible because he seemed so eager to please."

"That's right," she admitted. "While you argue about everything."

"I suppose I do," Rick admitted. "But it doesn't matter, because I happen to want the same things in life that you do."

Rebecca's throat constricted. If only she could be the woman he wanted those things with. Was there some point in their relationship at which she'd had a chance of becoming his true love instead of his friend? And if so, why hadn't she recognized it?

He stood up and moved away. Fear gripped

her, that he would walk out the door. She struggled to find the right words to stop him.

Before she could find them, Rick returned with the vase of roses and set it on a low table next to her. The rich old-world scent made her head swim.

He opened his shopping bag. "There were a few things I didn't want to give you in front of other people."

He wasn't leaving yet. Relief swept through her. "What sort of things?"

"I had a little trouble making up my mind," Rick said. "Let's start with this one." He handed over a package wrapped in silver and tied with a red bow.

Rebecca fingered the paper, reluctant to open it. She didn't want to give him any reason to depart.

Disappointment dampened his expression. "Am I making you uncomfortable? Maybe after what's happened, you'd prefer to be alone."

"No!" Feverishly, she pulled at the wrappings. It seemed to take forever to tear them off.

Out spilled a red flannel nightgown covered in white hearts. It reminded Rebecca of a sleep shirt she'd owned when they shared an apartment in their college days.

"It made me think of you," Rick said.

The fabric was soft and warm. And suitable for giving to one's sister, mother or aunt. "It's cute." After taking a deep breath, she added, "This is how you think of me?"

"As I mentioned, I had a hard time making a choice." He produced a second gift. "See if you like this one better."

Rebecca didn't hesitate. In a flash, she tore off the shiny red paper and white bow.

From inside, she lifted a red and black nightgown so slinky it nearly slithered right out of her grasp. The straps were thin and the lace semitransparent. "It's sexy."

"Is that a problem?" he asked.

It was, and it wasn't. She hoped he wasn't implying that they should continue having sex for its own sake. No matter how good it felt, she couldn't separate physical involvement from her need for love and security. "It depends on what you mean by it."

"That's the thing," Rick said as casually as if they were discussing what movie to see or where to eat lunch. "I didn't express myself very well yesterday. I was hoping to get another chance, but now that it's here, I'm having trouble finding the right way to say it. So is it okay if I just give you another present?''

"As long as it doesn't have red fur on it," Rebecca said.

"No fur, I promise." He bent over, trying to reach into the shopping bag, which he'd set on the floor. "Excuse me. This is a little awkward." From the couch, he dropped to his knees and, face averted, scooped something from the bottom of the bag.

"You'll get your suit wrinkled," Rebecca said. "Which reminds me, you must be late to work."

"I took the day off."

"That's a first!"

"This is a first, too." Rick held out a black velvet jeweler's box.

"What is it?" Rebecca tensed, expecting a practical joke. Did they make jack-in-the-boxes this small?

"The jewelry store didn't have a large selection." Rick regarded her with a shy expression that made her want to hug him. But he went on talking in that maddeningly impersonal way.

"Your tastes tend to be modern and mine are traditional, so I went with my gut instinct."

"About what?" she demanded.

"This." Rising to one knee, he opened the lid. A ray of sunlight from the window glimmered on a diamond set into a sculpted gold band. The design reminded her of a dove.

It was simpler, and at the same time more beautiful, than the one Steve had given her. That one had been chosen to impress other people. This one looked as if it had been picked for its own innate grace.

"Is that real?" Rebecca asked.

"The local jeweler is very reliable," Rick said. "We could have it appraised, if you like."

This conversation didn't make sense. This gift didn't make sense. "I don't understand," she said.

"I'm asking you to marry me," Rick said. "Aren't I doing it right?"

It wasn't like him to carry a joke this far. Or to make such a cruel joke, either. "Why?" she said.

"Didn't I mention that?" His cheeks reddened. "I'm in love with you, Becky."

She couldn't believe it. "Since when?"

"A long time, I guess, but I didn't know it," Rick said. "Yesterday was the first time it dawned on me, but by then you were mad at me. I decided to wait until today. It seemed more romantic, being Valentine's Day."

Any minute, he was going to clap her on the back and shout with laughter, then offer to take her out for ice cream. "I'm having a little trouble grasping this," Rebecca said.

"That's because you're afraid," he said gently.

"Why would I be afraid?"

"I was, too." Rick gazed up at her wistfully from his position on one knee. "Afraid of making a fool of myself. Afraid of losing you as a friend. Afraid we wouldn't get along because we fight so much. But none of that matters. I love you, Becky. We can get married any time you say, anywhere you like. I want to be your husband and your best friend for the rest of our lives."

He was right; she *was* afraid. Afraid she might burst into tears and spoil everything. Afraid he might change his mind, except she knew he wouldn't. "I can't believe I was so stupid!" she wailed.

"Excuse me?"

"I nearly married Steve! What did I have in my head, pencil shavings?"

Rick watched her anxiously. "Does that mean you're accepting my proposal?"

"Yes!" Prying the ring from its box, Rebecca slipped it on her finger. It was loose, but that could be fixed. "I love it."

"While you're at it, could you spare a few kind words for the groom?" he prompted.

"I love you, too." It was a relief to speak the words aloud. "You're wonderful. You're the man of my dreams. You don't still leave your laundry on the floor, do you?"

"I take it to the dry cleaners. Even my underwear," Rick said. "Can I get up now? Having a bad elbow is trouble enough. Another few seconds and my knee's going to give way."

Rebecca wasn't ready to let him up yet. There was something incredibly sexy about having a guy in a jacket and tie kneel in front her. Particularly a guy as handsome and well-built as Rick.

"I have a better idea," she said, and took hold of his tie. "Let's start here and work our way up."

His response was a teasing grin and a lightning upward attack to seal their betrothal with a kiss.

And, after that, a whole lot more.

CHAPTER SEVEN

A WEDDING IS ALWAYS a special event in Tyler,
Wisconsin. The marriage between the town's
former star quarterback and his longtime friend
Rebecca Salber was of particular interest.

The Tyler Quilting Circle had been working
for some time on a red and white quilt decorated
with red hearts, which was the ladies' gift to the
future bride and groom. It seemed almost as if
they had known that the couple would become
engaged on Valentine's Day and plan to marry
less than two weeks later in a heart-themed ceremony at the Fellowship Lutheran Church.

Quinn and Molly Spencer refused to take any
special credit for bringing the couple together,
although the romance had blossomed at their bed
and breakfast inn. "We're just glad it worked
out for them," was all either of them would say.
"It was a terrific weekend, really, all the way
around."

Football coach Pam Kelsey, who was known to be a mentor to Rick Travis, conceded only that she'd told him to follow his heart. And that she was glad for an excuse to buy a new dress to wear to the wedding.

The details of the forthcoming event were happily examined and approved of by the townspeople. True, Rebecca was wearing the wedding dress she'd bought for another man, but it had been altered and, besides, Rick was said to have a special fondness for it.

One of the bridesmaids, it was rumored, had spoiled the previous wedding. Apparently the bride had forgiven her. Perhaps even thanked her.

It was considered unusual and touching that, although there were three bridesmaids, the bride chose no maid of honor. Her husband was her best friend, she declared, and no one else could fill that position.

On such short notice, it was difficult, of course, to find a place for the reception. That might have explained the couple's decision to entertain their guests at Marge's Diner. Besides, it had always been the groom's favorite local hangout.

The couple would live in Rick's home on Gunther Street, and commute together to Madison. And, naturally, they would honeymoon at the Breakfast Inn Bed.

It was going to be a splendid occasion, and everyone looked forward to it.

REBECCA STARED INTO the mirror as Diane arranged the circlet of red and white roses atop her hair. "It's not exactly a perfect color scheme," she said to her mother.

Behind them in the church dressing room, the three bridesmaids posed for a photograph in their peach dresses. It hadn't seemed reasonable to ask them to purchase new dresses, even though these didn't go as well with the bright red heart theme as with Rebecca's former complementary choice of maroon. Still, the dresses looked pretty.

The trio smiled happily at Byron Forrester, the photographer. Ellen, Rebecca's fellow accountant, and health club friend Cindy had been terrific sports about the change in plans. Esther had been grateful to be included.

"Okay, the colors aren't ideal," Diane agreed. "And you know how I feel about having the reception in a coffee shop! But I'm learning to be flexible.''

"Everything's for sentimental reasons," Rebecca reminded her.

They both knew that what mattered wasn't the colors or the reception or the dress, although it looked lovely retrimmed with red hearts along the neckline and cuffs. What mattered was the groom. The right one, this time.

"That reminds me," Diane said. "I'd better go make sure Rick's here. His brother, Tony, was looking for him a few minutes ago." Tony served as best man.

Rebecca checked the clock on the wall. The ceremony started in fifteen minutes. "You mean Rick's late? He only lives half a dozen blocks away!"

"He's probably looking for a parking space. The whole area's jammed," her mother said. "Now stay here."

Rick should have arrived ages ago. Rebecca couldn't believe he would put her to so much worry on their wedding day.

"Becky?" Esther approached hesitantly. "I wanted to let you know something good that's come out of all this. Besides your wedding, of course.''

"What's that?" Rebecca hadn't entirely forgotten her old friend's cruel words or actions, but she understood the insecurity that had given rise to them. And her happiness was so great, she wanted to share it.

"Do you remember Jimmy Lafferty, who graduated from high school a year ahead of us?" she asked.

"He won first prize at the Science Fair," Rebecca recalled. "Didn't he wear horn-rimmed glasses?"

"Not anymore. He wears contacts," Esther said. "He's a computer programmer and he's been asking me out for the longest time. After seeing what happened between old friends like you and Rick, I decided to give him a chance."

"And?" she prompted.

"We had our first date last night. Becky, I've never enjoyed talking to anyone so much, except you, when we were younger," Esther said. "I really like him. Maybe it will work out."

"I hope so." Rebecca squeezed her hand.

Her other two friends approached, full of compliments for the charming town where the bridal couple would live. It was a few minutes before her mother returned, frowning.

"He's not here?" Rebecca asked in disbelief. What could have happened? Surely nothing would go wrong on her wedding day, not again!

She knew Rick wouldn't misbehave. He'd been loving and attentive and utterly delightful these past two weeks, even when her temper frayed over the details of rearranging her wedding on short notice.

He couldn't be suffering a change of heart. After all, it was he who'd pushed for the early date.

For one thing, he'd pointed out, she'd already agreed to give up her apartment and might as well move to his place. For another, they knew each other better than most brides and grooms, so what was the point of waiting?

Still, the fates did seem to conspire against her in the wedding department. Not that one disaster constituted a trend, exactly, but the first one had been spectacular enough to make Rebecca wonder if she was jinxed.

What could have happened to Rick? Yesterday after work, they'd shared supper in Madison, and he had picked up a last load of her possessions from the about-to-be-vacated apartment. That was eighteen hours ago, the longest they'd been separated since they got engaged.

She missed him. Surely he missed her, too. He wouldn't stay away on purpose.

"Maybe we should call the police," she said.

Diane frowned. "I think that's jumping the gun. Surely he'll show up any minute."

"He might be lying somewhere, injured and bleeding!"

"Or, if he isn't, he'll wish he were," teased her friend Cindy.

The humor brought Rebecca down to earth. Surely nothing serious had happened. Perhaps a flat tire...

"Hey! You can't go in there!" called someone in the hall. "The groom's not allowed to see the bride before the ceremony."

"It's an emergency." That was Rick's voice, out of breath.

Rebecca flew across the room and yanked open the door. "What emergency?" Her heart skipped a beat at the sight of him. His thick brown hair was mussed and his blue eyes bright with exertion. There was a fleck of blood on his white shirt above the red cummerbund. "Are you hurt?"

"No. It's not my blood." He gave her an apologetic grin. "I was almost late to my own wedding. Sorry, Becky."

She pulled him through the flock of fluttering bridesmaids and pushed him into a chair. "Now tell me what happened."

At the same time, she reached for a brush. That hair had to be tamed.

"I was coming out of my house when I saw the little boy next door fall and scrape his hands pretty badly on the sidewalk," he said. "He's only five, and his teenage baby-sitter got hysterical. I had to calm them down and get hold of the mother, and wait for her to arrive."

"You could have phoned," Diane said.

"I tried, honest," he said. "I called Becky's cell phone, but it's turned off. The church phone's been busy."

"That's true," Diane conceded. "I heard the secretary in the office organizing a pot-luck social." She examined the blood on the shirt front. "Now what are we going to do about that?"

Ellen rummaged through a desk drawer.

"Correction fluid ought to do it. Ah, here's a bottle!" She hurried to them.

The liquid dried to a pristine white. "That looks all right," Diane conceded.

"I'm sorry you were so worried, but I couldn't leave the kid in tears," Rick told Rebecca. "I kept thinking, what if he were our child? We'd want our neighbor to stick around, right?"

She nodded. She almost wanted to cry, she was so proud of him. "I'm glad you stayed."

"You two aren't agreeing on something, are you?" Cindy teased. Having hung out with them in Madison, she'd seen them squabble over almost everything. "I don't know if I can take all this peace and harmony."

"I consider it a nice change," said Diane.

After a rap at the door, Tony stuck his head in. A few inches shorter than Rick but of equally athletic build, he'd welcomed Rebecca into the family. So had their father, Albert Travis, a grizzled farmer whose words were few but well-chosen.

"Hey, bro, it's time to get moving," Tony said.

"On my way." Rick stood up, planted a glancing kiss on Rebecca, and strode away.

Diane lined up the bridesmaids and made sure they had their bouquets. She herself would be walking Rebecca down the aisle.

The foyer was clear of guests as the female members of the wedding party lined up. From within the sanctuary, a procession march began, and the bridesmaids stepped forward.

Becky clutched her mother's arm. "What if my knees give out?"

"Rick will catch you," she said.

"How about you? Won't you catch me?"

"Not if you knock me over," said her mother. "So don't do it."

Rebecca had never been so nervous in her life. She hadn't expected it. This was supposed to be a glorious moment, after all.

But the flurry of preparations had driven to the back of her mind the fact that she was making a commitment before her friends and family, before God and the people of Tyler. Now the realization hit her, full force, that for the rest of her life, she would be Mrs. Richard Travis, forsaking all others, cleaving only unto him.

It was a tall order.

Too soon, the organist began playing "Here Comes the Bride." Stiffly, Rebecca stepped forward on her mother's arm.

Then she saw him. Standing by the altar, Rick gazed at her with all the warmth of a crackling fire.

Memories flooded over her. Making microwave popcorn together in their college days. A night after the ballet when he'd parodied a pirouette and twisted a muscle. Tossing snowballs at each other during lunch break, and having to go back to work with her hair soaking wet.

How could she doubt for a moment that she wanted to marry this man? They were perfect for each other.

A moment later, her mother handed her to Rick and stepped aside. Next to Rebecca, he felt strong and steady. He was exactly the man she'd been looking for. All these years, he'd been right under her nose.

The pastor moved smoothly into the Lutheran service. Rebecca could only concentrate enough to hear snatches. "...God, who established marriage, continues still to bless it with his abundance..."

Maybe it was a good thing they hadn't rushed

into a relationship. They'd needed time to mature and to work out their differences.

When the pastor paused and nodded to them, Rick and Rebecca faced each other and joined hands, as they'd practiced last night. His large, warm hands had comforted a child today, she thought. Someday, she hoped, he would hold their own baby.

Repeating after the pastor, Rebecca said, "I take you, Rick, to be my husband from this day forward, to join with you and share all that is to come, and I promise to be faithful to you until death parts us."

"That goes double for me," Rick whispered. Grinning, he said aloud, "I take you, Rebecca, to be my wife from this day forward..."

Tony handed them their gold bands. They exchanged them, saying, "I give you this ring as a sign of my love and faithfulness."

At last, they prayed with the pastor. Rebecca could hear the townspeople, family and friends joining with them, and knew they were all treasuring this moment and this sacred promise. The light-filled church seemed at that moment to exist on a different plane from the ordinary world.

In all the years of her childhood, when she

had dreamed of her wedding day, she had focused on the flowers and her lovely gown, on the fairy-tale decor and the handsomeness of the groom. But now she understood that she had missed the best part.

It was the two of them joining together to walk through the years as best friends. Long after the flowers faded and the fine clothes were packed away, their love would continue to bloom.

Then the ceremony was over and the pastor presented the newlyweds to the congregation, who greeted them with cheers. Rick grinned and nodded while, out of the corner of his mouth, he said, "Let's go get a hamburger. I'm starving."

"How can you think of food now?" Rebecca demanded.

"I skipped lunch. Didn't you?"

Come to think of it, she had. "Okay, but..."

"If we hurry to Marge's, we can beat the crowd." Linking arms, he escorted her rapidly down the aisle and out into the crisp late-February sunshine.

"I need a coat!" she said.

"Not if we run!" Keeping a tight grip on her arm, he started forward.

Given no choice, she trotted beside him around the town square. People's faces lit up at the sight of the bride and groom and, when Rick waved, everyone waved back.

Afterwards, Rebecca realized how remarkable it was that Marge already had the hamburgers ready. "I know Rick," she said.

At the time, though, Rebecca was too busy chuckling to pay much attention. After being married less than five minutes, she mused, they'd already had their first squabble.

It was a promising start.